BIG BLUE ISLAND

By Wilson Gage and Glen Rounds

DAN AND THE MIRANDA
A WILD GOOSE TALE

By Wilson Gage

MISS OSBORNE-THE-MOP
THE SECRET OF FIERY GORGE
THE SECRET OF CROSSBONE HILL
SECRET OF THE INDIAN MOUND

BIG
BLUE ISLAND

Story by *WILSON GAGE*

Pictures by *GLEN ROUNDS*

THE WORLD PUBLISHING COMPANY

Cleveland and New York

J

11/65

Published by The World Publishing Company
2231 West 110th Street, Cleveland 2, Ohio
Published simultaneously in Canada by
Nelson, Foster & Scott Ltd.
Library of Congress Catalog Card Number: 64-19999
FIRST EDITION
COWP

For Jenifer Steele,
wit, playwright, and woman of the world,
from her mother,
who loves her tremendously all the same

BIG BLUE ISLAND

Mounting the hill, the truck went more and more slowly. The old man shifted gears and Darrell thought for a minute they were going to slide all the way back down to the bottom. But they made it at last and the engine, howling and snarling, pushed the truck up to the top.

The ground fell right away from the road and there was the river below, wide and winding and bright in the late October sunset. "Shoot," said Darrell, "it ain't anywhere near as big as Lake Huron." Not that he had ever seen Lake Huron to know it for sure. There was a heap of water around Detroit. Big old lakes everywhere.

He didn't say it aloud. He hadn't said a word to the old man since they left the bus station. He wasn't exactly scared of him. He just didn't much like him or want to talk to him.

They passed a house and then another house. The first house had a piece of an old Ford sitting in front of it and somebody had turned on a light inside one of the rooms. But the second house had a caved-in roof and a rotten porch. Nobody lived there, nobody had lived there for a hundred years.

The road dipped again and there weren't any more cleared fields, just woods. The dusk brought the trees closer to the road, big old gray smooth-barked trees, like elephants. Darrell stared back into the shadows. "Reckon there's bears in there," he said. "Woods like them must have bears in 'em."

Only he didn't say it aloud.

Of course, he didn't remember any bears around when he'd lived in Tennessee before. But that had been in town, in Knoxville, not out here in the woods with all these trees.

The road was unpaved and sometimes where a creek crossed it the water ran underneath but mostly it just ran over, making big splashy mudholes and ruts that gave Darrell the willies. If the truck got stuck he and the old man would never get it going again. They'd just have to sit here with the bears till help came.

But the road they turned off on was a hundred times worse. The old man didn't seem to care, he hit every bump and Darrell whopped his head on the roof about four times in succession. It wasn't really a road at all, just a place through the field where the grass had been mashed down by the truck going over it every now and then.

There was a rickety shack at the end of the trail and Darrell thought he'd never seen a worse looking house. But it wasn't a house. It was for the truck. There were a couple of doors standing open and the old man drove inside.

"Git out," he said. "And hurry. It ain't fixing to stay light for long."

Darrell pushed the door open and got out. He took his suitcase from the back of the truck and went out of the shack. He didn't see anything in the way of a house, not a

12

durned thing. There were the trees over yonder and a little below them the river, sucking at the muddy bank. A flat-bottomed rowboat was drawn up on the grass.

The old man closed the doors of the shack and padlocked them. Darrell just about laughed out loud. Who'd want to steal that broken-down truck? And if anybody had had a notion to, he could have knocked out one of the rotten boards, or squeezed through a crack.

Darrell still couldn't figure out where the house was. Might be the old man lived in a hole in the ground. Anybody who'd drive a truck held together by rust and lock it in a place like that shack most likely didn't have any idea about any kind of place to live. He'd live in a tent or a cave.

The old man set out and Darrell fell in behind him. There wasn't anything else he could do. I don't reckon it would be bad, living in a tent, he thought. Or a cave neither. Not in good weather.

But it was October. Already the wind off the river was cold. He didn't suppose down here in Tennessee they had snow and ice like in Detroit. Still it would be cold in winter. Had to be.

Darrell shrugged. It didn't matter to him. He didn't mean to stay here a mite longer than he could manage. By the time real bad weather came along he figured he'd be in Florida or Texas or some other place.

There was the boat. The old man shoved it down the bank and into the river. "Git in!" he ordered.

Darrell stared. He'd never been in a boat in his life. He figured he might not like it. That river wasn't as big as Lake Huron, but it was big enough. It was deep too. Anybody could see it was deep. And muddy.

"You live on the other side?" he asked nervously. He wouldn't have known the sound of his own voice.

"Naw," said the old man. "Make haste. Git in. It's fixing to get dark."

Darrell stepped into the skiff, leaning over and holding

14

onto the sides and sliding his feet over the muddy bottom.
The boat rocked.

"Set down there at the end," the old man told him.
"Don't fidget. I ain't used to having nobody else in here
with me, so you set still and don't get me flustered."

He sat in the middle and picked up the oars from the
bottom of the boat and pushed off. Darrell hadn't known
you had to turn your back on water to row over it. The
river slapped at the wooden sides and the oars splashed
gently. Darrell took a good grip on his wooden seat and
tried not to fidget. He wanted to ask again where the old
man lived, but he decided not to. It might fluster him.

Anyway, he'd know soon enough. It seemed a funny

15

thing to go out in the river in a boat, if you weren't going to the other side.

A houseboat? Maybe the old man lived on a houseboat. Darrell thought maybe that would be all right. He might just stay a while if he could live on a houseboat.

He looked over his shoulder. He couldn't see anything but trees. What a place to live, nothing but trees. It was enough to drive you crazy.

He turned back. The bank and the ratty old garage had almost disappeared. The old man bent forward and the oars dipped and then he swung backward on his seat till the brim of his straw hat nearly brushed Darrell's chest. Darrell could see the stringy muscles in his shoulders. The old geezer was strong. He must have been real strong when he was young. But Darrell didn't think he'd ever been young, he must have been stooped and weather-beaten and smelling of pipe forever, with all those gray whiskers that might have been a beard and then might not, poking out around his chin.

This was a mighty wide river. Darrell couldn't make out the bank at all now. Twilight smeared everything together into a gray haze. He had a scared feeling that maybe they were just going to go on rowing forever in the middle of all this no-colored nothing.

Suddenly the boat grated over something firm. The old man steadied the boat by digging an oar into the river bottom. "Jump out," he said.

Darrell stood up, wobbling a little. There was a lot of water between him and the bank, it seemed to him. But he jumped and only his heels landed in the river. It was muddy and oozy where he stood and he slid very slowly toward the water. He looked down at his shoes.

The old man's voice cracked in his ears. "You fixing to stand there all night? Lay hold of the boat and pull her in."

Darrell turned around then and laid hold. I could push him off, he thought. I could shove him out in the river and maybe he'd turn over and drown. But he just might not. He just might come after me with one of them paddles.

He pulled the boat up the bank. The old man got out and together the two of them pushed it up among the bushes.

"Ain't this the other side of the river?" Darrell asked. "How come you said we wasn't going to the other side of the river?"

The old man spat into the bushes. "Haw!" he said and Darrell figured that meant he was laughing. "It ain't the other side. It's the middle!"

Darrell nearly fell over in a fit. An island! They were on an island. He wondered how big it was. He listened hard and it seemed to him he could hear water running and gurgling all around him. It couldn't be very big. He wondered if the water ever covered it, in a flood, and what the old man did then. And where the heck did he live?

The island was a lot bigger than Darrell had thought. They walked through the half-dark for a long way and finally they reached the house. It was the kind of house you'd reckon an old man like that lived in, no paint and the roof sagging and panes of glass out of the windows.

The old man opened the door and the smell of fried things and kerosene and pipe tobacco and musty clothes came right out of the house into the cold night. The smell was strong and lonely and it made Darrell uneasy. Inside the old man struck a match and lit a lamp on the table.

Darrell's eyes bugged out. No electricity! No lights, no TV, not even a radio!

"You might as well be one of them bears back in the woods," he said scornfully. Not aloud, though.

The room was low-ceilinged and moderate-sized and tidy. Things were old and ragged and not too clean, but the dishes were all stacked neatly in a cupboard, the bed in the corner was made up nicely with a quilt drawn up to the pillow, and the floor was swept.

"I got a cow to milk," said the old man, picking up a lantern and lighting it. "You set down and wait. I'll be back in a spell and we'll eat."

He went out and Darrell sat down on a high-backed straight wooden chair. There was an armchair by the stove, but anybody could tell the old man had sat in it so long it wouldn't fit anybody else.

Darrell shivered. It was cold in this gloomy place. He reached inside his jacket and drew out a smashed ham sandwich and three damaged chocolate bars. He hadn't had to spend a cent for food on the bus, people had given him things left and right just for looking pitiful. He'd bought all this and some comic books and a pocketknife and a fluorescent pink tie in Nashville, spent all that the Relief people had given him to eat on. And now he was sorry. If he was going to get to Florida, he was going to need money.

He ate the ham sandwich and wished he had a Coke or an Orange Crush to go with it. He ate two of the candy bars but he couldn't manage the third one. He was thirsty and looked around for some water but he didn't find any. The chocolate glopped up his tongue so he could hardly swallow.

18

Still the old man didn't come back. Darrell sat there in the yellow light of the lamp that breathed out and in like a person and wondered what he was going to do. He'd made his first mistake not leaving home as soon as he was sure his momma was going to die. The Relief people never would have got hold of him then. He'd never have ended up here in the middle of nowhere.

But he couldn't have left his momma. Not the way she looked, so thin and big-eyed and hoping. Not after his daddy had run off and left both of them.

In a way he couldn't blame his daddy. There he was, with no car and no job and Momma sick, and the people coming to take back the TV set and the chair and sofa covered with red plastic that felt almost like cloth and could be wiped clean with a damp rag. His daddy had been out of work for over a year and they weren't getting any more compensation when he left.

Darrell hadn't exactly hated to see him go, he'd got so mean you couldn't blink your eyes he didn't throw a shoe at you. But he'd been scared to be by himself with his momma the way she was. She wouldn't see a doctor till the State Relief people made her and then it was too late. She was so T-betic she didn't live a month after they took her off to the hospital. By that time the Relief people had him in their claws and knew he had this old great-uncle living down here in Tennessee, somebody to take care of him, they said.

The door opened and the old man came in. He had four eggs in one hand and a bucket of milk in the other. "Reckon we can eat now," he said.

"Not me. I ain't hungry," said Darrell.

The old man shrugged. "Suit yourself," he answered. He made a fire in the big range and the room began to warm up. Darrell had to take off his jacket after a while.

The uncle stirred himself up some kind of mess on the stove and made some coffee. "I'll take a cup of that coffee," said Darrell.

"Naw, you won't," the old man answered. "There ain't enough but for me. Coffee costs good money and there ain't any point wasting it on young 'uns. It ain't good for 'em no way. You can have some milk."

Darrell said okay. He was thirsty and he didn't care about the coffee. When he got to Florida, he'd drink coffee all the time.

The milk was good. It didn't taste like any milk Darrell had ever drunk before, and when the old man filled his glass a second time, he just let him.

There was a sink in one corner and water came out of a pump. Darrell hadn't known what it was. He could have gotten himself a drink of water if he'd known. The old man heated a bucket of water and washed up the dishes. Darrell yawned. He was tired. He'd spent two days and a night on the bus.

The old man put his cup and saucer in the cupboard and shut the door. "I'm fixing to go to bed," he announced. "Reckon you'd better go too." He picked up the lamp and crossed the room to open a door.

There was a second smaller room behind it. The old man used it for storage, Darrell could see. Big tin cans full of something stood against the wall. A fat sack of meal and a tumble-down dresser and some stacks of old newspaper, among other things, fell within the circle of light. And there was a cot, made up fresh with sheets and blankets.

20

"Come cold weather," said the old man, "you'll have to sleep in the big room. You can sleep in here till then. I don't like having folks in the same room with me when I'm sleeping. Besides, I snore loud enough to wake the dead. I don't reckon you'd like that. Now git over to the sink and wash up."

"I ain't dirty," said Darrell.

"I don't keer," said the old man. "Folks wash afore they go to bed. And you do it too."

Darrell washed. The old man gave him the lamp. "You holler when you get in bed and I'll come get the lamp," he said. "You're likely to turn it over and set the place afire."

With the lamp gone the only light was the slit under the door. Then that too was gone, and Darrell heard the old man muttering to himself as he climbed into bed. It was black as pitch, Darrell could just make out the faint outline of the one window.

He lay in the cot still as a stone. How was he going to get away from here? He had to get away. In Detroit he never went to bed till he durned pleased. All night long the lights from the street had shone in the windows of their place and the sound of cars and voices drifted up. How could he live in this place, with no electricity or TV or movies or people or nothing? How could he go to bed with the chickens in the jet-black dark?

He could hear the clock ticking in the next room and every now and then the harsh growly sounds of the old man's snores.

He'd get away from here and get to Florida. He didn't know how, but he would. Florida would be fine, it would be wonderful. His daddy always talked about going to

21

Florida, back in the days when he had a job and they lived, all three of them, lived happily in the apartment in Detroit. He closed his eyes on the hot stinging feel behind them.

CHAPTER 2

WHEN DARRELL woke it was light. He got dressed and hung his pajamas on a peg, just like he'd worn them instead of sleeping in his shorts and T-shirt. He went to the window and stared out, but all he saw was nothing. Gray fog pressed its flat eyeless face up against the glass and looked in at him. He didn't like it.

He poked around a little bit in the room, squinting into boxes and taking the lids from the big tins. They were full of corn. He opened the drawers of the rickety dresser. There was nothing in them but rags and paper. Mice had been after the paper and it was all in flakes.

He was hungry. He couldn't tell whether the old man was up or not. He listened for a long while and it seemed to him he could hear sounds in the other room. At last he pushed the door open.

The old man was gone. The bed was made and there was a fire in the stove. There was sunlight somewhere, it came through the windows softly because of the fog. Darrell went over to stand by the stove, because the other room had been cold. The clock ticked in its sad steady voice

23

and the fire every now and then whispered and muttered. It seemed to Darrell he must be all by himself a million miles from nowhere, and he was lonely and scared in a way he had never been before.

The door to the outside opened and the old man came in with the milk. "Well, you're up," was all he said.

He poured some of the milk in a jar and the rest in a crock. He put some wood and coal in the range and poked at the fire a little bit. When he'd slammed the stove shut, he turned to Darrell and said, "I'll get you some breakfast. But after this you got to get up when I do, else you'll have to do your own cooking."

Darrell shrugged. "Okay," he said.

The old man could cook, Darrell would say that for him. He fried an egg the way it ought to be fried, with the yolk so hard it didn't run at all. And he didn't spare the sirup on the bread. And that milk was good.

"I'll hot up a dab of water," the old man said. "You wash up them things and dry 'em and put 'em in the cupboard. I got work to do."

Darrell just sat there looking at his plate, and the old man went out. As soon as the door closed, Darrell jumped up and went to the window and watched the old man trudging off. He picked up his plate and glass and stuck them behind the stove. Then he scooted out the door and took off.

The fog had just about thinned out. The sun spread through it in a glow. Darrell stared around at the trees. He couldn't say he'd ever really liked trees, but these were mighty pretty, red and orange and yellow, with a scatter of dark green prickly trees like Christmas trees.

He got some of the little evergreens between him and

24

the house and barn. Now when the mist all went away the old man couldn't see him. He hoped it went away soon. He wanted to look this place over good and see what the island was like and what would be the best way to get off it.

The boat was the best way. He didn't know whether he could row or not. It didn't exactly look hard when the old man did it, but sometimes things that looked easy as pie turned out to be the hardest things to do, like playing the guitar.

He figured the river must be just ahead of him. He walked quickly and soon he could hear it beyond the bushes. He ran forward and then something happened that nearabout startled the juices out of him.

As he busted out on the bank, a thing—a big enormous thing with wings—leaped up in front of him and flapped off over the water muttering and growling to itself. Darrell was too scared to yell. He gave a jump that shook him to his heels and one foot gave way under him. He went down on his knee and stared after that thing. He'd seen all sorts of sights in his lifetime, he'd seen a dead whale once and a rocket the Air Force shot and a picture of a man from India with a white sheet all swaddled up around his middle. But he'd never seen anything like this.

There was something unnatural about this place. All those trees and the stillness and now this thing. It couldn't be a bird. The spread of its wings was wider than he was tall, by a good bit. There weren't any birds like that except in outer space or something. And birds didn't make noises like that. He could still hear it off over there somewhere, grumbling to itself.

It didn't make him feel too good. In fact he turned around to go back to the house. And then he decided he had to

get away from this island, so there wasn't any use being
scared. He made up his mind to go on. He was stuck down
here with all these bears and crazy things till he could find
a way to get loose and headed for Florida. He'd have to
use the boat to get off the island, he knew that. All the
swimming he could do was dog paddle and not much of

26

that. It was his bad luck to end up on an island. Other places he could have just sneaked out the window and found a highway and thumbed a ride, anywhere in the wide world he wanted to go.

The bird or whatever it was was gone. Darrell didn't see or hear a thing. He made up his mind to go look for the boat. There was a kind of path along the river, someone had cleared it, cutting away undergrowth here and there. Darrell followed it till he came to the point where the boat had landed the night before.

It was gone. He knew this was the place. He could see the signs in the mud, the imprint of his own feet and the old man's and the marks where the boat had slid up the bank and into the weeds.

Maybe it had floated off in the night. He wondered if Old Whiskers had another one. If he didn't, would they have to stay here till somebody rescued them? And who would ever come along here, away back of behind the tail end of nothing?

He clenched his fists. He had the worst luck! And he was too dumb to know when good luck came along and tapped him on the shoulder. All that way from Detroit, he could have got off the bus anywhere. Oh, the driver and some of the folks would have looked for him for a while, but he could have got away. Especially during the night when the bus stopped, he could have slipped out of the station and been gone long before anybody knew.

He hadn't even thought about it. He didn't know why, he'd just got back on the bus and let it take him right here, where he might as well be dead and buried.

He squatted and stared for a long time into the moving water, marbled with green and brown. The ripples hit and

hit and hit against the shore till the rhythm almost put him
to sleep and he had to jerk away from it. He stood up and
walked back along the path. He noticed a splash of orange
paint on one of the trees and wondered what it was.

He found some shells on the river bank. Paired shaggy
shells like brown wings, joined with a little gluey piece of
something. Inside they were beautiful, smooth and pearly,
every color of the rainbow. He thought they must be some
kind of special shell. They were so beautiful they must be
valuable. He slipped them into his jacket, feeling happier.
He could sell these shells, somewhere, and make money to
get to Florida with.

He had come to the end of the path. And there was the
boat, in the water. For a minute he thought he'd got turned
around and that this was the spot where they'd landed.
Then he remembered the footprints. Naw, the old feller
had moved the boat up here. It was chained to a ring in
a tree by a big rusty padlock. The old man believed in lock-
ing things up.

Darrell examined the lock. He didn't think he could bust

it or pull that ring loose. He'd have to steal the old man's keys sometimes when he wasn't looking. He pulled the boat up to the bank and stepped in. It sure wobbled a lot. He picked up one of the oars and stuck it in the water. He didn't know how to hold it right and it was heavier than he'd expected. He'd never be able to manage two of them.

All right, he'd get in the boat and let it go. He'd take some food and a blanket and let it drift down the river. For all he knew the river just might run on south to Florida.

It was a good idea. He couldn't wait to try it. But he didn't have food or money—except the shells—or any way to get the boat loose. He'd have to bide his time if he could stand it.

He went on around the end of the island. At the very tip the little waves came at him, one after another, from all directions. The sun hit on each one and glinted up at him. It made him dizzy and he turned and headed back toward the middle of the island. He went through some trees. They were big old trees and for a minute he felt a little like he might get lost. But he went on and then there was a field, with a scrawny cow in it. She was eating grass and she never looked up when he went by. It was a good thing. He didn't know much about cows. He'd as soon not have anything to do with this one.

There was the back of the house. It wasn't easy to see among the bushes, it was so squatty and gray and uneven. Around at the front half a dozen ratty looking chickens pecked sadly at the muddy ground and scattered as he came up. He went inside. The old man was sitting at the table eating dinner. There wasn't any for Darrell that he could see.

Now wasn't that something? The old man was going to try to starve him to death.

"Ain't I going to get nothing to eat?" he asked angrily.

"You wasn't here," the old man answered peaceably. He took another mouthful of green beans. "'Sides," he went on, "there ain't but this here plate. I figured you must have took the other one and high-tailed it out of here. I couldn't find it nowheres."

Darrell said nothing. The beans and fried meat looked good. He couldn't help staring at them. And corn bread. He couldn't remember how long it had been since he'd tasted corn bread.

The old man chewed and chewed. He got up and took a bowl of stewed pears off a shelf and spooned some out.

Darrell couldn't stand it. He didn't care what the old man thought anyway. He got the plate and glass from behind the stove and took them to the sink and washed them. The beans and meat were on the stove, and a pan of corn bread. When he sat down, the old man gave him two big spoonfuls of the pears.

"Git you some milk if you want it," he said.

They sat there and ate together and Darrell began to feel almost friendly toward the old geezer.

The old man pushed his plate back and took up a toothpick. "You come a long way, from Detroit," he said finally. "It's a good piece from Detroit to Tennessee."

"Longer coming back than it was getting there," said Darrell. He didn't really remember much about getting there. It had been more than three years ago.

However he could remember plain where they used to live, in Knoxville, in a neat house on the side of a hill. His momma had a washing machine and it stayed out on the front porch. He could remember how on summer nights they would sit out on the porch and watch the drive-in movie at the bottom of the hill. They could see the big picture easily, though they couldn't hear the words. Darrell's daddy said he could figure out what was going on if he watched often enough.

Daddy worked at the hosiery mill, and every now and then Momma would work too, for a while. When Momma was working, lots of nights they'd get in the car and go down the hill to the picture show. Darrell didn't think it made much more sense when you could hear the words and mostly he slept on the back seat. But Daddy always bought him a couple of candy bars and a Coke as big as he was.

Then the hosiery mill closed down and Daddy heard about work in Detroit. Darrell remembered how it had been at first in Detroit. He and Momma had been scared all the time. They didn't know how to get around or anything and people weren't friendly. He grinned a little. What a punk kid he must have been then, scared by a few cars and people!

His daddy hadn't been scared. Right away he'd got a good job and they'd bought the TV set and all. Even Momma would have got over being scared and lonely if she hadn't got sick.

It hadn't taken Darrell long to learn his way around the neighborhood. He got friendly with three other boys from Tennessee who lived there. Pretty soon they knew how to get to most any place they could walk to. After Daddy lost his job and couldn't get another one, Darrell had spent a lot of time just walking up and down the streets. He didn't like to be home too much when Daddy was mean and Momma was sick.

Well, that was over and done and here he was in this crazy place. He didn't think he wanted to go back to Detroit, not ever. But there were lots of good places in the world. He wanted to be in one of them, in a town where things were going on, not stuck in the middle of a muddy river way out in the sticks.

"I been to Chicago," the old man said suddenly. "Been to Chicago, Louisville, and Evanston, on the train, twice. Couldn't hardly wait to get back here."

Darrell was surprised. He hadn't ever been any place but Knoxville and Detroit and he hadn't ever been on a train at all. He didn't know what to say. He turned his head and stared out the window.

And there was that thing! It was walking around by the barn, big as you please, long-legged and long-necked, with

32

a great long sharp bill and a long feather sticking out the back of its head.

"Looky yonder!" he gasped. "What the heck's that? Look at that big thing!"

The old man shifted his toothpick. "After mice, I reckon," he said. "They come around the barn once in a while after such. Not rats, I ain't got no rats. But I got mice."

"What is it?" insisted Darrell. "Is it a bird? Ain't it too big to be a bird?"

The old man grinned. "You don't know much, do you?" he asked. "Everybody round here knows them cranes. Big blue herons, game warden calls 'em."

Darrell let that pass. He watched the bird amble along, pecking at the dirt almost like the chickens. The old man coughed. "Tell you what," he said. "You catch one of them fellers and I'll give you a dollar."

Darrell swung his head around and narrowed his eyes. "You mean that?" he asked.

"Sure do," answered his uncle.

"Is that the only one?" Darrell wanted to know. "The only one now," the old man said. "There'll be eight, ten more before the winter's over."

A dollar. Darrell figured he wouldn't have another chance to earn a red cent stuck here in this two-bit place. It ought to be easy. He could catch a big thing like that easy, with a rope or fling a rock at it or something. Then he'd have a dollar in his jeans when he headed for Florida.

"Dead or alive?" he asked.

The old man grinned again. "Dead or alive," he answered.

CHAPTER 3

Dᴀʀʀᴇʟʟ ʜᴜɴᴋᴇʀᴇᴅ on the river bank. "How come I can't go?" he shouted. "How come I got to stay here?"

The old man swept the oars through the water and the boat shot out over the brown river.

"On account of I say you can't," he answered shortly. He pulled up the oars and rested them on the sides of the boat and the current carried him gently downstream. That was why he had that path along the river bank, Darrell knew now. He set out from the top of the island and strong as he was he still couldn't row straight across because of the current. That place where he landed, where the truck was kept, was slantwise across the river from here. And when he rowed back, the current pushed him further downstream, to the low end of the island. The old man walked along that path with a rope tied to the skiff and towed it up to the head again, so he could warp his way back across the river next time he left the place.

Now he sat and let the boat drift. He seemed to be thinking. "I got business to do," he said finally. "I can't be bothered with a kid, I'd get flustered. I won't be gone more'n four or five hours." He thought another minute. "I'll fetch you something," he added.

He thrust the oars back into the water and began to row. Darrell picked up a stone and skipped it over the water. He didn't exactly throw it at the boat, just sort of alongside. The old man didn't even look to see. Anyway it was only skipping, not real throwing.

Darrell stood up. He didn't want to go anyway. The old man wasn't going into the town, not the big town where Darrell wanted to go. He was headed for some little whistle stop where they probably had two stores and a gasoline pump. Darrell would as soon stay here as go look at it. He wondered what the old man could bring him from a place like that. Whatever it was, he wouldn't take it. It wouldn't be anything he'd want.

The old man was halfway across by this time. "I wouldn't of gone if he'd asked me to," Darrell muttered. It was just being all by himself on this island with all those trees and that old cow and a couple of nutty birds. Darrell never had liked being by himself for long. And especially not in a place you couldn't get away from, like an island.

It was a warm day, plain hot in the sun. It was dry too. There'd been no rain for a long time. The old man had put out the fire in the stove before he left and screwed the matches up in a glass jar and hid it somewhere.

"If this place was to catch on fire, it'd go up like a cane-brake," he said. "It ain't I don't think you got good sense enough not to strike a match, it's just I know too many folks with good sense that's laying dead in the graveyard right this minute. Things happen."

35

Darrell didn't care. He had a book of paper matches somewhere in his suitcase, if he wanted to look. Now he followed along the path beside the river. In the night they'd let water out of the dam a few miles below and a wide strip of cracked mud and slimy rocks lay where yesterday ripples and minnows had chased each other.

As Darrell walked he could hear something plop in the water ahead of him, a series of quiet splashes, one after another.

It was turtles. The first time he'd seen them, clustered on the bank half on top of each other, like scales on a fish, he couldn't figure out what they were. "Turtles," the old man said. "Sliders. Warm weather brings 'em out. They'll climb up on most anything to set in the sun."

Darrell didn't like the look of them. Some of them were as big around as a bucket, or bigger. And there were thousands of them. Suppose somebody fell in the river, those things would eat him up in no time. The old man said they weren't the biting kind of turtle, but there was plenty the old man didn't know. Darrell had thought once about learning to swim real good and swimming to shore, but he put that thought out of his head after he saw the turtles.

He got down on his hands and knees and began to crawl. It was the only way he'd found to get close to them. Even so, he didn't get very close. One of the biggest stuck up

its scrawny head and gave him a look and then slid off into the river.

The biggest ones always went first. The little ones let him come near enough to see the yellow stripes on their necks before they tumbled in. "That's how come you see so many more old 'uns than young 'uns," the old man pointed out. "Little 'uns set there and let 'emselves get killed. There's a heap of things in this world you don't get two chances to learn."

Darrell glowered. He got plenty of chances to teach the old man a thing or two, like how to shut up. But he never dared do it somehow.

He had a good chance now. He had half a mind to do it. He could go back to the house and find those matches and set fire to the place. That'd teach the old geezer. The whole place would burn—house, trees, barn, fields, everything. He'd have to get out in the water to save himself, but the water wasn't deep along the bank. He could get down in it with just his head sticking out and . . . and the rest of him down in there with all those turtles. No, thanks. He'd think of something else.

He looked up and there, right in front of him, was that big old blue-gray bird with its mean-looking beak and its snaky neck and long legs. Darrell drew in his breath. He'd been after it over a week now, to get that dollar, and he'd only glimpsed it a couple of times, skimming over the water grumbling to itself or sitting in a tree way down at the far end of the island. And now here it was almost alongside him.

There were a lot of good throwing rocks around here, he'd seen them. Where were they now? There wasn't anything he could reach but little old pebbles. There! Over

37

there was a good one. Cautiously he stretched out his arm
and put his hand on it. It was round and just the right
size. Darrell grinned a little. He was a good thrower, he
was bound to get this big old bird.

He raised his arm and let fly and he hadn't any more
than let go than he wished he hadn't. He should have got
closer. He was pretty good at throwing, but not down on
his knees this way, and that little narrow head wasn't much
of a target.

The stone whizzed by the heron. The bird turned its head quickly this way and that, looking startled, and then flew. When it flew, its neck curled in on its shoulders and its great legs dangled. Darrell could see water dripping from its big scaly feet.

The bird didn't fly far. Forty yards down the river it settled back in the shallow water. It folded its wings neatly around its body and stood still as a statue. Darrell hadn't known anything could stand so still. The plumy feathers on its head stuck straight out in back.

After a while it lifted its foot and scratched briskly at a place near its shoulder. Then it smoothed the feathers with its bill, over and over. It took two solemn steps and stood once again frozen into absolute stillness.

Darrell didn't think it could see him. He crept slowly along the path. It wasn't so hard on his hands, but rocks cut into his knees right through his blue jeans and made him cuss a little. He would have earned this dollar if he ever got it, he'd say that.

Suddenly the heron bent its head and darted its big beak out and caught something. Darrell watched. When the bird straightened up it had a good-sized fish. Darrell thought the bird wasn't going to be able to hang onto its catch, the way it kept shifting the thing around with the fish flapping its fool head off. But the heron was pretty smart. It got the fish's head inside its beak and squeezed hard and the flapping stopped.

Still that was a mighty big thing to go down that skinny neck, Darrell figured. The heron seemed to think so too. It held its head up high and wheezed a little bit around the fish and appeared to be considering how to get it down.

39

Then it shut its eyes and drew in its neck a little and gulped and the fish vanished. Darrell was interested to see a big bulge slide slowly along the bird's slender neck.

The heron stood still a few minutes looking a little dazed as though it was making sure it hadn't split anywhere or busted anything. Darrell felt around and picked up another rock. He was peeved with himself. He should have thrown while the heron was swallowing instead of sitting there with his eyes bugged out watching. He bet he could have got it easy then. Now it was walking off slowly and sedately, looking from side to side with those curious sharp quick movements of its head.

He threw again. The stone grazed the bird's wing and with a honk of surprise the heron picked itself up and flew off toward the end of the island.

Darrell ran. He pelted down the path and around the end of the island. The heron was standing halfway up the other side, in water so deep it looked as if it was floating on the river like a duck. Darrell raced on, and out of some bushes right beside him a heron suddenly flapped up, so close he could feel the wind its great wings made. It scared the daylights out of him and for a minute he kept on running out of sheer fright. The first heron saw him then and made off over the little brown waves, flying so low its feet almost dragged in the water.

"Two of 'em," Darrell muttered. "I didn't know there was two of 'em." He remembered then what the old man had said, that there would be eight or ten around before the winter was over. So here were two of them. He gritted his teeth. That second one had been so close he could have laid a hand on it if he'd only known it was there. He could have reached over and grabbed it by the neck.

40

He walked slowly back to the path. Maybe that would be the best way, to catch one in his hands. Sneak up through the bushes and jump on that old bird. It would be hard. But he knew now that he was never going to hit one with a rock, he couldn't throw that good.

He came out on the path and stopped dead. Three of them! They ranged the shallow water along the island's edge, still and straight, each one rising from its own image in the water.

I can catch one of them, I know I can, he thought. But as though he had shouted the words, the nearest bird took flight. Its long wings swept slowly up and down as it sailed up the river.

Bushes almost hid the second one. I can get him, Darrell told himself. I can crawl in under the bushes and grab him by his legs.

It took a long time. He crept quietly, quietly, inch by inch. The heron was still there, he could see the top of its head as it stood motionless in the water. If he could get through those bushes without scaring it, he'd be close enough to spit on it.

It was muddy under the bushes. Gnats and mosquitoes hummed around in there like it was July instead of early November. He squirmed along on his belly. At least the mud didn't make any noise, not like gravel or dry leaves. The gnats sang in his ears. He could see the water and the bird's thin legs straight ahead of him.

He made a lunge and had one of the skinny gray things in his hand. His face went underwater but he held on for dear life, gasping and sputtering. The heron didn't move.

It was a little tree of some sort, a slender gray-barked

tree trunk he held in his hand. A curly blue-and-white feather rocked on the ripples and that was the only sign of the bird. No telling how long it had been gone.

He was mad clean through. And wet. He'd have to go get on his other pair of blue jeans. He never had been able to stand sopping around in wet clothes. He walked back to the house with his jaws clenched in fury.

The little house looked empty. It was a funny thing about a house like that, how you could tell there wasn't anybody home just by looking at the outside.

He stood on the doorstep and when one of the chickens went by, he said "Hi" to it just like it was a person. It was lonesome here. He hated it. He didn't want to go inside. Somehow it was even lonesomer inside.

Finally he opened the door. His dinner was sitting on the table, cold biscuit and sausage, cold turnip greens, and the can of sirup. He was hungry, but he didn't want to eat in here.

He wished that clock wouldn't tick so loud and steady. It made him gloomy to hear it. He wished there was a fire in the stove. Fire noises were cheerful. He wished Samuel, the cat, was in here. He liked Samuel, a big old gray-and-white Tom with one bad eye. But the old man said Samuel wouldn't come in the house till after Christmas. It must be true. Darrell had brought him in yesterday when he found him in the barn and the cat had all but clawed the door down getting out.

Darrell opened the door into the storeroom. It was so quiet he could hear the beat of his own heart, as loud and melancholy as the clock's tick. He changed his clothes quickly and went back into the other room. He'd take his dinner outdoors and eat it. At least there were chickens and birds to keep him some sort of company.

He put out his hand to pick up his plate and then he stood there, as still as one of the herons. There was somebody outside! He could hear it plain. Somebody was sneaking around outside the house!

CHAPTER 4

H E KNEW NOW what people were talking about when they said their hair stood on end with fright. His prickled up all over the back of his head. Who in the world would come to this place? Nobody who was up to any good, he was certain.

The footsteps were right outside the door. "Run!" Darrell told his feet. "They ain't nobody to come help you. If you don't run you ain't got a prayer."

But he couldn't move. His hand was still stuck out over the biscuits. He just stood there like a bush rooted to the worn linoleum, and the door swung open.

When the man saw Darrell he jumped a foot and dropped the bucket he was carrying. "Good Lordamercy!" he yelled. "I didn't know there was anybody here."

"What you want?" Darrell gasped. He grabbed up the sirup can. He could throw that. He wished he'd thought to run over and get the poker.

The man stooped and picked up the bucket. "Did I scare you?" he asked. "You sure scared me. I never thought there was anybody here. I seen the old man's boat was

44

gone and I never counted on anybody else being here."

"What you want?" Darrell asked again.

The man gave him a funny look. "Water," he said shortly. "Did you think I come to rob the old feller? What's he got you think anybody would want?"

Darrell relaxed a little. He guessed that was right.

The man came on in and went to the pump and filled

his bucket. "I come by here three or four times a year, maybe more," he explained. "I even spent the night here one time. But mostly I just stop for water from this here well. I don't mind drinking river water just plain, but I don't like it for making coffee. It kind of spoils the taste. All that mud in it, I reckon."

He picked up the brimming bucket and turned toward the door. Then he stopped and looked at Darrell. "You the new hired hand?" he asked doubtfully.

"Naw," Darrell answered quickly. "I'm just visiting. I'm—he's my uncle."

"Is that right?" said the man. "Well, I reckon he's glad of a little company. He don't have what you might call a lot of it. How come you ain't in school?"

Darrell didn't mind telling him. The newcomer seemed friendly enough. And since he got off the bus ten days ago, he hadn't said a blessed word to anybody but the old man.

"We was living in Detroit," he said, "and my momma, she died. She had TB. And my lungs—" he laid a hand on his chest "—my lungs was dark or something." He had a picture of his lungs in his mind. They were shaped like two inner tubes and they were jet black. "Doctor said I had to wait a while before I went back to school. Didn't bother me none. I never did go to school too much."

"Oh," said the man. "Well, I'm sorry. About your momma and all." He looked at the table and the plate of food. "Put them biscuit in a sack and come on down to my boat. I'm fixing to eat dinner and I'd be happy to have some company."

Darrell didn't need to be asked twice.

The man's boat was a flat-bottomed wooden boat, like the uncle's skiff, but about three times as big. It had a

46

kind of roof made of a sheet of canvas stretched over four poles, one at each corner of the boat. On one side there were two more poles. They were really small tree trunks, cut just above the point where they divided into two main branches. Slung into these two crotches was a long wooden rail from which dangled a series of short chains with curious slender metal branches at the ends.

Darrell had never seen anything like this. But in the center of the boat was still another pole with a windlass and cords attached to that rail, so the rail doubtless got lowered into the water and pulled up for some purpose.

"You a fisherman?" asked Darrell. He'd seen all kinds of fishermen in all kinds of boats since he'd been on the island. But not one like this.

"Reckon so," answered the man. "I'm after mussels so I reckon that's kind of a fisherman."

Darrell stared. "How come you don't do exercises or something?" he asked. "How come you go fishing to get muscles?"

The man stared back. "How else would you get 'em?" he wanted to know. "They're down there on the bottom and there ain't but one way to get 'em up." He looked confused. "Oh, I see. It ain't them kind of muscles, like in your arm. It's this here kind of mussel." He reached over and picked up a thing like a rock and held it out to Darrell. It was two rough brown shells, shut up tight like a book or a purse. Darrell knew what it was. He'd been right to save those shells he'd found, he thought with a little thrill of satisfaction. He'd known right away they were valuable.

"There's a thing inside there, like a snail—or a oyster, more like, I reckon," the man went on. "But it ain't no good for nothing. It's the shell that's worth money."

47

Darrell almost whooped out, he was so excited. He had one pair of shells and he felt certain he could find more. He wouldn't need to catch that old crane. He'd be rich enough to *buy* Florida.

"You get a lot of money for 'em?" he asked.

The man nodded. "I get a good price for pigtoes, like this," he answered. "Right now price is running about a hundred fifty dollars for a two-hundred-pound bag. But they ain't easy to find no more. Pistol grips and butterflies is what I get mostly."

I might of known, Darrell thought grimly. Nothing good happens to me.

But he'd hang onto that shell. It was mighty pretty and anyway, maybe this man didn't know everything. Maybe there was something special about his shell that would make it worth more than a couple of cents . . .

They sat down and Darrell opened his sack and drew out a biscuit. The man had already filled the coffeepot and set it on a little three-legged cookstove full of hot coals. The stove stood on a piece of metal nailed over the bottom of the boat.

The coffee began to boil. "Once I kicked over that stove and set the boat afire," said the man with a grin. "I had a time putting it out."

He got out two cups and filled one from the pot and offered it to Darrell, along with a paper sack of sugar and a tall can of evaporated milk. "Take all the cream you want," the man said, holding out the can. "I got another can here. I like to have plenty."

He had plenty to eat too. He had sandwiches—bologna and cheese—and bananas and cold baked sweet potatoes and doughnuts and a whole store-bought cake with cherry

48

icing. He shared it all with Darrell and Darrell ate till he nearly popped.

"Looky yonder," said the man suddenly pointing with half a sweet potato. "There's one of them blue peters."

"One of them what?" asked Darrell. He glanced up and discovered what the man was pointing at, a sort of gray duck with a black head and a white bill. It was swimming along the edge of the island in little quick spurts, darting its head back and forth as it swam.

"Blue peters," repeated the man. "I don't know how come them to be called that. They ain't blue, they're black. Or gray maybe. Come cold weather, they get together on the river, a whole big raft of 'em, maybe a thousand. When they see me coming, mostly they move off. But once in a while I can sneak up and scare 'em, and then it's a sight for sore eyes. They spread them little wings out and run over the water like it was solid ground before they fly off." He took a bite of sweet potato and looked thoughtful. "Reckon that's why they're called blue peters. Peters anyway. Because they walk on the water like St. Peter in the Bible."

Darrell wasn't much interested in blue peters. They were just ducks, sort of, and nobody had offered him a dollar to catch one. He looked around the boat. "Is that your motor?" he asked, nodding toward the end of the boat.

"Yeah," answered the musselman.

"Can it go fast?" Darrell wanted to know.

"There ain't no need to go fast when you're brailing," said the man, and he sounded a little put out at Darrell's question. "It's a good motor though. It don't never conk out. I don't never have to be towed home or anything."

He went over and started the engine. "You want to brail with me a while?" he asked.

49

"Sure," said Darrell, though he really didn't know whether he did or not. Maybe brailing was hard.

The man eased the boat away from the island and out into the river. Then he cut the motor and the boat began to drift. He lifted the rail with its dangling chains from its resting place. "This here's a brail," he explained. He pointed to the little slender pieces of metal at the ends of the chains. "See these hooks? Fifty of 'em. There's been times I brought up fifty pigtoes on that one brail. But not lately."

He dropped the brail into the water and the windlass turned as the cord reeled out. The boat turned almost sideways to the current and began to move faster. After a while they left the island behind and the boat slowed a little. "We go along like this, real slow, see, and the brail goes along close to the river bed. All them hooks just barely drag. Anytime one touches a mussel, it grabs a-holt, snap! like that, see. And it holds on till I bring up the brail."

Darrell nodded. Brailing wasn't hard.

They drifted on. Darrell ate the rest of the doughnuts. He was beginning to like being in a boat. The sun was warm and the wind over the river was just cool enough. The musselman talked about how he used to have a partner. But they couldn't make enough money for two. The other man had quit. "He went to work for the Esso station," said the fisherman. "And then he bought a car and went to Texas. He was crazy to go to Texas. I been there. Florida's the place to go. But he was a pretty good mechanic and mechanics make good money in Texas. Anyhow since he left I ain't made no more money than before. Mussels are scarce. And it's mighty lonesome work. There's days I'd just as soon go to work at the Esso station myself."

Darrell changed his mind about asking for the partner's

50

job. A motorboat passed them headed the other way, and after a while another.

"Them nuts," said the musselman in disgust. "They ain't trying to make a living. They're fishing for fun."

"Where're they coming from?" asked Darrell. A third boat was coming toward them, close enough to make the skiff really bounce in its wake.

The man pointed across the river. "There's a motel up there," he said. "You can see a piece of it if you look good. A real nice motel and a café. Lots of fishermen use it. The highway comes closer to the river right here than any place else except the dam and that's five miles on down."

"What highway?" asked Darrell.

"I forget the number," the musselman answered. "Goes down to Birmingham, you know? And on south, New Orleans, maybe. Must be ten trucks an hour going by on it."

"You going over on that side?" Darrell tried not to sound excited. But if the boat went near that other bank, he could sure jump out and find that highway. Trucks would almost always give you a ride. Once he got to Birmingham, wherever that was, he could decide what to do next.

The musselman shook his head. "I fished that side last week," he said. "Ain't a mussel in the place. Anyway we got to get back."

Darrel said nothing. He never had any luck. But it probably wasn't such a good idea to set out without any money. A boy in Detroit had told him as long as you had a dollar in your pocket the police couldn't arrest you for hitchhiking. It might be true.

He'd get that old crane and collect that dollar. And now

51

he knew where to head. He'd hit that highway soon enough.

The musselman was hauling up his brail. Six brown shells clung to the lines. The musselman swore and pulled them off and threw them in a basket. He turned the boat and lowered the brail again and started the motor.

Ahead of them there was something on the water. Something flying low over the river, raising and lowering its great wings in slow even beats and every now and then sailing gently for a while with its long legs trailing out behind it.

It was a nice thing to watch. Darrell hadn't noticed before but there was something about the rise and fall of those wings that was—pretty, somehow. He didn't know exactly how to say it, and anyway he wasn't fixing to say it. But he liked watching.

"You ever see many of them?" he asked.

The musselman nodded. "A good many," he said. "If I throw out mussel meat, all kinds of birds come around. Those that don't come to eat come to see what the commotion is about. But mostly I don't throw it out. I can sell it to a man makes canned cat food out of it. Lots of years I wouldn't make a living without catfood."

Darrell wasn't listening. "You reckon you could get one with a rock?" he asked finally.

The musselman stared at him. "One of them big blue cranes?" he exclaimed. "You better not try. There's a law against it."

Darrell wondered why the musselman would think he was dumb enough to believe that. Why would there be a law against killing a bird? Nobody would care enough about a bird to make a law about killing it.

"Who'd know about it if you did it?" he asked finally.

"The game warden would," answered the musselman.
"He's on and off that island and up and down this river all
the time. He and your uncle are friends, sort of. And what's
worse, that's part of the Reserve, where you live."

"Part of the what?" asked Darrell.

"Don't you know nothing?" the man demanded. "The
reserve, where nobody can't shoot or trap or kill nothing.
All that orange paint on the trees, that's what that means."

53

Darrell had wondered about those splashes of paint.

"You can go to jail for quite a spell if the game warden picks you up for something like that," the musselman went on. "Me, I got no hunting license or duck stamp or crane stamp, and I don't look cross-eyed at nothing like that. Them's federal laws."

"I ain't scared of no game warden," Darrell said sullenly. But he thought maybe he was. He stared down into the brown water foaming away from the sides of the boat. The old geezer must hate me as much as I hate him, he thought miserably. He was aiming to get me in trouble and have me put in jail. Seems like there're easier ways to get rid of me than that.

It was a jolt. He just hadn't got around to figuring maybe the old man didn't want him. How come him to say he'd take me when the Relief people wrote? wondered Darrell. How come he just didn't say no?

When the musselman let him off, Darrell started to ask for the loan of a match. He was pretty sure he'd lost those paper matches. The old man would be sorry when he came home and found the place burned to a cinder.

But he couldn't think up a good enough lie. He just stood on the bank and watched the musselboat go off. He didn't want to go back to the house. He didn't think he could stand listening to that clock.

The old man was halfway across the river before Darrell noticed him. He ran and hid in the bushes and watched his uncle go by with a lot of bags and bundles. Wonder what he brung me, he was bragging so about, Darrell thought.

He stayed in the bushes but after a while it got shadowy. It was creepy around here at night, the water noises and the silence in between and the bears and all. Darrell knew there weren't any bears, it just *felt* like bears.

He went back to the house and after a while he looked in a window. There was a carton of Orange Crush and a box of vanilla wafers and a Milky Way on the table. That must be what the old man had brought him. It wasn't so crazy. He sort of wished he'd gone on in and taken them when the old man first got home.

But it wasn't till the old geezer had opened two of the Orange Crushes and swallowed them down that Darrell got mad enough to go inside and help himself.

CHAPTER 5

T HE OLD MAN got up next morning and cast a calculat-
ing glance at sky and river and announced, "No rain today."

Darrell wasn't anxious for it to rain. He wasn't looking
forward to being penned up in the house with the old
geezer. He had half a mind to move out in the barn with
the cow. He sat staring out the window.

"What you sulking about?" the uncle asked finally. "You
act mean as a cat with its tail caught in the door."

Darrell went on staring. The old man pulled a couple of
baskets out of the storeroom. "Whatever ails you, you can
work it off," he stated. "You and me got to pick apples.
Once we get some rain, it'll freeze, and I don't want them
apples to freeze."

Darrell sprang up. "You can pick apples," he cried. "I
ain't going to. It ain't my job."

The old man shrugged. "Suit yourself," he answered.
"But you ain't going to get no vittles till you do some work,
and you can count on it."

He picked up his baskets and went out. Darrell stuck
out his tongue at the door as it closed behind him. When

the sound of footsteps had grown faint, Darrell began to scrabble frantically through the cupboard and along the shelves. The old man meant it, he was sure of that. He'd see a boy eleven years old lie out on the floor and die of starvation before he'd give in. As soon let him starve as go to jail.

There wasn't anything to eat. There were some turnip greens soaking in a kettle and a big sack of raw cowpeas by the stove. Even the corn bread left over from breakfast had gone to feed the chickens, crumbled in a pan with some stale buttermilk. There was a hunk of salt pork in the cupboard, and two jars of pears he couldn't get the tops off. He took the jars in the storeroom and hid them. It had only been an hour since breakfast, he wasn't hungry. But he'd be hungry by night. He'd break the jars then and eat pears. And maybe some of the corn meal out of one of the big tins in here. He wasn't looking forward to it.

He sat down on his bed and stared around at the walls. The whitewash was crumbling off the boards and spider webs hung down in big tangles from one corner. This was the awfullest place in the world, he guessed. It didn't seem real that he was stuck here in this crummy dump. It just wasn't right.

Bad things were always happening to him. Everything was against him. He didn't deserve it. He jumped up, clenching his fists and breathing hard. He wished he had somebody to fight or something. He picked up the end of his cot and banged it hard on the floor four or five times.

The cot was heavier than he had thought. When he quit banging it he was panting. He sank down on it and buried his face in his pillow, gritting his teeth.

There was a hard gnawing pain in his side, where maybe

he'd strained his guts lifting the cot. Or maybe he was hungry. He *was* hungry. He was awful hungry. He was dying of hunger, starving, starving. He felt lightheaded and dizzy with hunger. By night he'd be dead.

It was better to go to jail. At least in jail they fed you. He was going to have to catch that old crane and go to jail and he hoped it was soon.

But he had to have food. He couldn't live, much less catch that bird, without something to eat. He'd have to go pick apples. He sat up.

Besides he ought to pay for his food. Even if he didn't want to be here eating the old man's corn bread and sleeping in this cot, here he was and he ought to pay for it. His daddy always said, "Don't take favors." Anyway he wasn't going to take charity from somebody who hated him enough to send him to jail. He had that much pride.

The apples trees were down at the far end of the island, past the barn, past the garden where there were still a few rows of beans growing and some turnips, and past the cornfield, fenced in to keep out the chickens and the cow. Darrell glanced at it scornfully. It wouldn't be much trouble picking apples if the old man did it the way he gathered corn. It looked like he'd left half of it.

There were about six apple trees, small and gnarled. The apples were pretty good, though. Darrell had already sampled them. The old man was standing on a bucket picking steadily. The trees were so undersized he could reach almost to the top branches.

He didn't turn around. When Darrell had been standing there a minute, he spoke. "Pick up them apples on the ground," he said mildly, "and put 'em in that other basket. If they got a little rotten place in 'em, take 'em. But if they got a big rotten place, leave 'em for the coons and the yellow jackets."

Once again Darrell stuck out his tongue at the old man's back. He got the second basket and went to work. The yellow jackets hadn't waited for word they were welcome. They were swarming all over the place. Darrell was scared skinny of them. He wasn't going to let on, though. He snatched in and out among them and seized the apples. Once he picked up an apple and its underside was all rotten and the little gold wasps were burrowing everywhere in it. When he saw them Darrell gave a squeak and flung the apple as hard as he could.

The old man just went on working. After a while he got down from the bucket and came over to look in Darrell's basket.

"Ain't I told you to leave them half-rotten ones?" he asked fiercely. "They ain't worth picking up. Now watch what you're at or I'll wallop you a good one."

He sorted out half a dozen apples and tossed them on the ground. He didn't seem to mind the yellow jackets at all.

He's mean as they are, Darrell thought. They're probably scared to death of him.

The old man climbed back on his bucket. The sun was hot and the sky was hazy. A big tug went slowly up the river, on the far side of the island. Darrell could see it through the trees. He wondered where it was headed. I'd sure like to be on it, wherever it's going, he thought.

Four or five crows followed in the wake of the tug. They discussed the news among themselves in flat husky voices, as they flapped along over the water. They saw the apple pickers and three of them came over and gave some help-

59

ful advice. Darrell couldn't help grinning at them a little. They were just like some people he knew.

But they were big. He wondered if all crows were as big as these. He hadn't known how big they were before he came here to the island.

The old man moved his bucket over to the next tree, and Darrell scuffled around in the tall dry grass and weeds. The grasshoppers sprayed out on each side of him like drops of water. They clung along the weed stalks and stared out of their big dull eyes.

Darrell put a couple of the best apples in his shirt, in case the old man decided not to feed him anyway.

It took the biggest part of two days to gather all the fruit. They put the good apples in the barn, in a bin full of straw, but Darrell's culls they brought into the house. It was drizzling rain as they carried the last basket inside. It seemed to please the old man.

"Got 'em all in," he said with a grin. "I don't like to work myself up into a lather over them apples, but this time it worked out real fine. We got 'em in, you and me, and now it'll turn cold."

Well, who cares? thought Darrell.

He stared out the window. In Florida it never rained or turned cold. Things were going on there all the time, movies and car wrecks and bank robberies, the lights stayed on everywhere all night and people danced and sang. In a sudden rush the rain swept toward the house and the bushes and trees bent before it. From some hiding place under the eaves, a jay flew up and out into the wind, making a sudden desperate plunge into the misty sky. Drops bulleted against the pane.

The clock ticked.

60

The old man got out a kettle and began to peel apples. He cut them into quarters and dropped the pieces into the kettle with little dull thuds. The wind banged at the windows. In the stove the burning coal shifted softly and spoke for a moment in thick hoarse whispers. Darrell sprang up suddenly from his chair.

"Ain't there two knives?" he cried. "Can't I do some of the cutting? I can't hardly stand sitting here not doing nothing."

The old man cut his eyes around at his nephew. "Changed your tune, ain't you?" he asked drily. "Just a while back you was willing to do without meals before you'd do a lick of work."

Darrell turned sullenly back toward the window. He might have known. Being in school, being in jail, being *dead* was better than being shut up here with the old geezer.

The old man stood up. "I got another knife," he said. "Glad for some help. I reckon you can use a knife all right? You won't cut yourself or nothing?"

Darrell gritted his teeth. "I ain't a baby," he said finally.

He took the knife and moved his chair over by the old man's. He peeled the best way he knew how, to prove to the old guy that he wasn't any dummy. He cut out the bad spots carefully.

"You going to eat these?" he asked at last.

The old man nodded. "Make us a pie for supper," he said. "I'll stew the rest of 'em down with sugar and molasses and make us some apple sauce. When that's gone we can start on the ones in the barn. My momma, she used to dry apples, but I forget how she done it." He put down his knife and picked up his pipe and sucked on it. "I used to

pick apples when I was your age, helped my grandpa get all kinds of fruit, pears and apples and stuff like that to put up for winter. Picked berries. I wish I had a nickel for every gallon of blackberries I picked. Once I was picking blackberries and I come on a big rattler, big around as my leg, swallowing a rabbit. Rabbit's legs was still hanging out of its mouth."

Darrell didn't know whether to believe this or not. "What'd you do?" he asked at last.

"Didn't do nothing," said the old man. "I was too scared and flabbergasted. I just stood there and the snake went off. Say, you're pretty good at peeling. You ain't cut yourself at all."

Darrell glared and the old man grinned. He put down his pipe and took up his knife once more. After a while he said, "My momma used to put cobwebs and soot on a bad cut to stop the blood. But my wife liked to use kerosene."

"Your wife?" repeated Darrell, astonished. "You got a wife?"

"Had one," said the old man. "She died, four or five years after we was married. I was working for the railroad then. I never did like it. And she died and we didn't have no children so I quit the railroad and wandered a little. Then I come back here and bought this farm and been here ever since."

"How come you to choose this place?" asked Darrell, really wanting to know. Why would anybody make a choice to live in this place?

"Like it here, I reckon," the uncle answered. "Nobody around to bother you. And my folks was living down the river then. My ma and pa was dead, but I had a couple of sisters and a brother. Now they're dead too, and my wife and all. I ain't got anybody."

He went on peeling. Darrell turned his head and watched the weeping world outside. "I guess you're like me," he said finally. "I ain't got anybody either."

CHAPTER 6

THE RAIN went on and on and on. When Darrell woke up in the mornings he kept his head under the covers as long as he could, so he wouldn't have to hear it smacking down on the roof. He dreaded it.

It was awful being shut up in that house with the old man. There wasn't anything to do or any place to go except around and around each other. They brought in the wood and coal from a little lean-to. Every day the old man milked the cow and Darrell hunted up the eggs. But mostly they just stayed in the house and peeled apples. Darrell nearly went wild.

The worst was when the old man did the washing. He picked the wettest day yet and washed some sheets and a couple of blankets and every living stitch Darrell owned. They squeezed the things out and hung them up on ropes all around the room. Darrell had to sit in a chair wearing nothing but a ragged old sweater of his uncle's that nearly itched him to death. The clothes weren't wrung out too well and they dripped and dripped inside while the rain dripped and dripped outside. The fire roared and the place steamed up till Darrell could hardly breathe and he hoped he drowned.

"Ain't there anything to do around here?" he burst out finally when he'd sat for half an hour listening to all that dripping, and scratching and squirming around inside the sweater.

The old man took his pipe out of his mouth. "Naw," he said. "Not till them clothes dry. The apples are all done. I'm fixing to do some reading. I could get you something to read."

Out of the storeroom he fetched a great pile of papers, a couple of old almanacs, and a stack of ancient *National Geographic Magazines*. Darrell hoped there'd be some comic books in the lot, but there weren't. The funny strips in the papers were the best he could find. He read them all.

The old man concentrated on the newspapers too. He looked over every page. Once in a while he'd mutter the words under his breath. What he seemed to enjoy most was the little fillers at the bottom of the columns and he read these aloud to Darrell: "'The Veterans Administration has been an independent agency of the United States Government since 1930,'" he read. And then a minute later, "'It is estimated that forty thousand people die from snake bite every year.' Think of that!"

Darrell raised his eyes from Dick Tracy and thought about it. "Any snakes on this island?" he asked uneasily.

"I reckon," said the old man. "I don't see too many, but there's bound to be a good many."

Darrell turned back to Dick Tracy. But it went through his head suddenly that the old man wasn't scared of anything, not snakes or wasps or the river and floods or being out here alone and not anybody around for miles and miles.

65

I bet he'd be scared of some of the tough guys in Detroit, thought Darrell. Like the ones he'd seen waiting for the bus one time. The ones that might have been carrying knives or guns. He'd been scared himself, but not very much. Not as scared as the old man would be, he reckoned.

They sat there for three days in the steamy house waiting for all the clothes to get dry and the rain to stop. Darrell read all the funnies twice and then he started in on the *Geographics*. They weren't bad. They had good pictures, in color. He looked at all the pictures and then he decided to try an article about sharks. It was pretty good if you skipped the hard words.

The old man went on with his reading. Darrell learned a lot. "Brazil produces half of the world's coffee." "Petrels and some other sea birds lay only one egg. Sea gulls usually lay three to a clutch."

Well, who cares? thought Darrell.

"Here's one for you," the old man added. "'In some urban areas two per cent of all crime is committed by boys under the age of twelve.' I reckon you're kind of glad you moved away from Detroit. You might of got in bad trouble if you'd stayed."

"I can get in bad trouble right here," squalled Darrell suddenly jumping up. "I guess you ain't so glad I left. I guess you're just waiting for me to get in trouble and go to jail!"

The old man stared at him over the top of the newspaper. "I don't know," he said finally. "I'm supposed to be taking care of you. I reckon if you was to do anything real bad, I'd be the one that'd have to go to jail, seeing as you're under age and all." He dropped his glance back to the paper. "Anyway you get in trouble and you'll see what happens. I'll wallop you good."

With a trembling hand Darrell picked up his magazine. "I reckon there ain't no way to get in trouble stuck out here in the middle of the river," he said sullenly. But there was a way. He knew it. And he might not get his dollar but he'd get to see the old man hauled off to jail and that would be durn near as good.

When the clothes were dry at last, the old man coiled up the ropes and put them away. Darrell watched. He knew where the ropes were and he knew where the herons were. He could see them out the storeroom window. Eight of them perched in two trees at the top of the island, looking bored and dignified while the rain streamed down all around them. Once in a while they shifted around, once in a while one of them stroked wings and breast with a great wicked-looking bill. But mostly they just sat.

He liked seeing them there when he looked out. It was a lot better than just seeing trees and river. It was like seeing a friend, somebody you knew, anyway.

And it gave him something to think about, planning how he'd tangle the ropes around and catch one. Or make a noose and lay it on the ground and sit in the bushes till one of the birds stepped inside the loop. Then he'd jerk the rope quick and catch that big old crane. It made prickles run down his back to think about catching one of them, one of those great big strange-looking creatures. He bet not many people had ever done a thing like that. Maybe he'd get his picture in the paper.

The rain ended little by little, with the sky growing gradually lighter and the wind steadier. Going to the barn Darrell had to hang onto his jacket to keep it from getting blown clean off him. He could see the white caps running along the river, going the other way from the current. They were like some kind of animals crawling over the water. He watched for a few minutes and then ran on into the barn. His teeth were chattering. It was as cold as Detroit.

That night they had frost and the old man moved Darrell's bed into the front room. Darrell lay awake for a while. It was noisy—the old man's snoring and the fire and that clock. By and by all the sounds blended together; he hardly heard the racket, and finally he dozed off.

What he thought about before he fell asleep was how he was going to have to get up before the old geezer some morning soon and sneak those ropes out of the house. It seemed like an easy thing to do, only somehow he couldn't manage it. One night he woke and heard the old man still snoring away, though it was nearly morning, he could tell by the feel of things. He poked his head out of his blankets thinking now he'd do it, but the air was so snappy and cold and it felt so good in bed, he just went back to sleep.

And then about a week later he got his chance. The old man shook him awake before it was light. "Git up," he said. "We got to get started. We're fixing to go to town."

Darrell's back teeth nearly fell out. He hadn't figured his uncle would ever let him cross the river.

He got up and began to dress.

"You eat now," the uncle ordered. "I'll tend to things in the barn. Then you wash your face and hands good and we'll leave."

He was hardly out of the door before Darrell was cramming his breakfast down. He was still chewing his corn bread when he got the ropes and opened the house door. He ran past the cornfield and down along the river bank to the place where he'd first seen the heron. That was the spot to try to trap one, he'd decided.

He didn't try to make a noose or net because he didn't want one of the birds to get caught while he was gone. He had the ropes out of the house at last and that was a good start. He stuffed them under a bush and they kept spewing out in coils and loops. He pushed them back in on one side and they kept coming out on the other. He was frantic for fear the old man would come back to the house and find him gone. He grabbed up some dry leaves and sticks and hurriedly covered the ropes. Nobody came down here anyway. Nobody would see.

He ran back to the house but he didn't quite make it. He met his uncle right at the door.

"Where you been?" the old man asked. Darrell didn't know what to answer, so he didn't say anything. "Ain't I told you to hurry? What you out here for? And you ain't washed your face! Now make haste."

As they moved out over the river the sun was halfway shining. The wind was nowhere near as strong as it had been the past week or ten days. Darrell looked back at the island. He wasn't exactly crying his eyes out over leaving the place. Even if he was just going to spend the day in some crummy little dime-store town, he was glad. He'd had about all the trees and chickens he could stand.

The town was even worse than he expected. The street was wide and had big trees along it, even in the block that must be the business section. Two filling stations, a ten-cent store, a drugstore, and the bank ranged along it.

There were Christmas decorations strung overhead, ropes of sad-looking red and green lights and a few dusty silver bells. Darrell had forgotten it was near Christmas. He didn't care. He hadn't had anything like Christmas since Daddy lost his job and it hadn't hurt him any. Anyhow what kind of fun could people have when they lived in a dump like this?

Still, somebody in town must know something. There were four or five late-model cars parked along the main street. They were so sleek and shiny they almost made Darrell homesick for Detroit. There was even a Cadillac parked in front of the bank.

They went to the bank and to the doctor and to the ten-cent store. Darrell didn't like any of it. The bank was a skinny brick building with a skinny glass door, an old cheap-looking place Darrell figured probably didn't have ten dollars in it altogether. He figured it had probably never been robbed. Nobody would think it was worth robbing.

The doctor had hard hands and cold instruments and didn't mind letting you know it. He looked so deep into Darrell's ear it felt like he must be looking out the other side, and made his patient stick his tongue out so far he could have curled it around his ankles.

At the dime store they bought Darrell some clothes, jeans and shirts and a jacket, all miles too big for him. He didn't care. He wasn't fixing to wear anything the old man bought for him anyway.

The salesgirl knew the old man. They talked a little and when she handed Darrell his package she said, "How you like it, living out there? It always seemed like it would be kind of exciting living on an island."

She and the old geezer stood there staring at him till finally he had to say, "It's all right."

They ate lunch at the drugstore. It was a pretty good drugstore. Darrell had been in lots worse places than this in Detroit. It smelled right too, like a city place, of vanilla ice cream and medicine and cigars and fried potatoes.

He sat up at the counter and ordered a cheeseburger and a double Coke and a piece of pecan pie. Real food. It was just like being in Detroit or Florida or any place. He stared at himself in the big mirror back of the counter. Reflected in it the street outside and the cars and even the silver bells looked better.

The old man talked to the druggist and Darrell finished his lunch first. He wandered over to the magazine rack and looked at the comics. They were mostly "The Katzenjammer Kids" and the "Classic Comic of Ivanhoe," not very good. But even "Nancy and Sluggo" was better than nothing. He wished he had some money.

71

It was late when they got back to the island. They put the truck in the shed and hauled out the two big cans of kerosene and a bag of groceries. There were lots of groceries left in the truck.

"We'll get these things over," said the old man, "and you can take 'em in the house and I'll come back here for the rest."

Darrell shrugged. It wasn't any of his say-so. When the boat scraped up on the island, he dragged out one of the cans of kerosene and headed for the house. He was tired and hungry. The farm seemed friendly and familiar now that he was back here. It surprised him. He guessed it was because of all that long dull day in town.

It was a pretty evening. Behind the thin skin of clouds in the west the sun was setting. The river was bright with it and a fish jumping made flashing rings over the water. Darrell liked the way the light fell in long yellow streaks over the cornfield and the barn. It made everything look strangely clean and different. The wind hardly stirred and in a tree two crows talked together in slow grating voices.

Darrell turned to look at them. And there against the wide gold field of the sky he saw three of the herons coming home to the island, gliding, tilting their bodies and wings gently to catch the air currents, dropping slowly, slowly toward the trees. Huge and dark, they landed with big slow flappings in the top of a sycamore and shuffled into their favorite places.

One of them shook itself and its feathers suddenly stood away from its body. It looked bigger than ever, strange and awkward. And then just as quickly its feathers closed around itself and it began to stroke them and smooth them with its bill.

72

"Them old cranes!" said a voice right behind Darrell, and he jumped like a rabbit.

It was the old man.

"I thought you was going back after the rest of the things," Darrell said angrily.

"I was going to," the old man told him. "But I figured we both needed our supper. Them things will be all right over there. I'll get 'em first thing in the morning."

When Darrell woke, the room was full of sunlight and the old man wasn't anywhere about. Darrell sat up in his cot and looked around. It must be halfway through the morning. There wasn't a sign of breakfast on the table or the stove. The room was cold and when he opened the range and looked in, the fire had burned down to ashes.

He poked it up a little and added wood and coal. The old man didn't let him mess around with the fire much, and he took his time, putting on the small logs and chunks just to suit himself. He clanged the door to finally. The room didn't seem so empty with the fire roaring.

But all of a sudden he was worried. The bed in the corner wasn't made up. Where was his uncle? The old geezer always woke Darrell as soon as the meat was frying for breakfast. How come he'd let the day get this far along without even making his coffee?

Darrell dressed in his old jeans and shirt and opened the door to look out. Frost powdered everything and under the white winter sky the world lay pale and brittle. When he stepped onto the grass the stems cracked under his feet and behind him his footsteps appeared, dark and wet.

He went to the barn. Mattie the cow was still there. She looked up at him when he came in. She didn't like him, he could tell. She always looked at him so mean. Well,

74

he didn't like her either. But the old man hadn't been out here or she'd be out in the field.

"Hey!" Darrell hollered and there was a stir of birds in the roof. All of a sudden he was scared. He was all by himself here, deserted, forgotten, left behind. He'd go get the boat and try to get to shore.

He ran out of the barn. He didn't know where the boat was. Down there where they'd landed last night? He went that way, running past the cornfield.

There was something lying at the edge of the field, a big darkish lump. Darrell almost yelled when he saw it. It was the old man. He was dead, he'd died out in the weeds and left Darrell all by himself in this awful place!

CHAPTER 7

D ARRELL stood by the bed looking down at the old man. How long would it take the two of them to starve to death, he wondered, stuck out here in the river with the groceries back there on the other bank? The cow had gone dry and even if she hadn't, Darrell wasn't fixing to try to milk her. Eggs were getting scarce. The patch of turnip greens lay colorless and limp under the frost.

The old man opened his eyes and looked up at him. "Don't look so gloomy," he said and grinned. "I ain't dying —yet. My back's just stove up some. I'll be all right in a week, maybe two, three weeks."

"What we going to eat while you're getting all right?" demanded Darrell. "We ain't got no milk nor hardly any eggs and all them things you bought are over yonder."

The old man looked up at the ceiling. There was a long spell when he didn't say anything. Finally he said, "See them two bricks back of the stove there? Set 'em up on top so's they'll get hot."

Darrell found them and did as he was told. He poked up the fire and added some coal. "We ain't got much coal," he pointed out darkly.

76

"We got wood aplenty," answered the old man. "You can chop wood, can't you? And we ain't going to starve, we got meal and salt meat. We got apples and pears, green beans and tomatoes I put up myself. And there's turnips out there for you to dig. Be a few good ones left anyway."

He stirred a little and groaned. "Fetch me that bottle of liniment up by the clock," he ordered. "And we'll get an egg or two right along. We ain't got much coffee now, and that's bad. I get mean without my coffee. And we ain't got no milk. In a way it's a lucky thing Mattie ain't giving no milk. Who'd milk her? Not you. You're scared of her. Bring me them bricks."

Sullenly Darrell took a piece of dirty flannel the old man held out to him and wrapped the bricks in it.

"I bought enough canned cream for an army, but it's in the truck," the old man said, after he'd groaned around trying to get the bricks against his back just the right way. "If you could row, you could get back over there and get it."

Darrell busted out then. "If I could row," he yelled, "I'd get in that boat and go on off. I'd just leave you here and you could die, for all I care! You could just lie there and starve."

He broke off, a little bit scared by what he'd said. But the old man just grinned.

"What you so sore about?" he asked, still grinning. "Go on off if you want to. I been like this before and I managed. I ain't dead yet. I can git along without you as good as you can git along without me, or a lot better."

Darrell clenched his fists. He was so mad he felt as if he might just blow up and scatter into a million pieces. "I guess you couldn't of got along without me so good this morning," he shouted. "You might of just laid out there in the grass and froze if I hadn't come out and dragged you in."

"I was making it," said the old man calmly. "Takes more than a heavy frost to kill me." He shut his eyes and looked like he might go to sleep. But after a while he spoke again. "Anyway, I'd be all right this very minute if somebody hadn't left all them fool ropes out there in the bushes for me to fall over."

He opened one eye and said sharply. "That was you, I reckon. Ain't nobody here but just us two, and I wasn't the one did it, I'm certain-sure."

Darrell just stood there like a ninny with his mouth hanging open. He'd long since forgotten the ropes. And the herons and the dollar for that matter. Oh, he wished he had that dollar. He wished . . . he wished . . . anything, anything except being here in this place with this old uncle.

The old man watched him a minute and then heaved himself over in bed, groaning and grunting. "Put them bricks back on the stove. And get me that bottle of cough medicine, down there under the sink. Big, tall bottle, way in the back."

"What you want cough medicine for?" asked Darrell. Not that he cared. He just wanted something to say. "How come you want cough medicine? You ain't got no cough."

"You be quiet," said the old man.

It was freezing cold. Darrell opened his mouth to take a big gulp of the frosty air and it rushed into his mouth and made his teeth ache savagely. He said "Wow!" and went on toward the barn.

The wide doors swung open with a long wail from the hinges. Something at the back of the barn made a scuffling

78

noise and Darrell had a glimpse of a fat gray behind and a long scaly tail vanishing into the shadows. He knew what it was. A huge old possum. The old man kept talking about how he was going to trap it and eat it, but he never had.

It looked just like a big rat to Darrell. He didn't know whether he wanted to eat any of it or not. When I first come here, he thought, I'd of had the liver scared out of me if I'd seen that thing. I'd of thought it really was a great big rat.

He brought Mattie out of her stall and across the barn-yard to the field back of the house. He didn't have to do it, she knew the way. But taking her there made him feel like he was ordering her around. It made him feel like maybe he wasn't scared of her and her sharp horns and her mean eye.

Back in the barn Samuel came and bumped his head against his legs and Darrell stooped to stroke him. He didn't fool himself, Samuel was hoping for some milk, that was all. Still it was nice to have the old cat around to talk to and Darrell scratched the round head gently in appreciation.

He cleaned out Mattie's stall carefully and then he fed the chickens a handful of grain. He could do all these things better than the old man could. He could get along without the old man any day in the week. He could live out here all by himself as long as he wanted. He didn't need any-body, and the old man could put that in his pipe and smoke it.

Of course, he hadn't yet got the hang of making corn bread. But he would. He took a fork and went to dig turnips. The ground was like iron and finally he had to fetch a pick. Even using the pick it was hard. When the point struck the ground, the shock jarred him to his toes.

And the very first thing he did was drive the tool right through a turnip.

It didn't matter. It was all withered and worn-out looking. Frostbit, maybe. You could probably get poisoned from eating frostbit turnips. Still he tried to be more careful. If the old man didn't get better soon, they were going to run out of corn meal and canned tomatoes.

He got warm digging. He stood up and unzipped his jacket. All around him the cold blue day was still and quiet. The sun was up over the trees and the river smoked a little in the chilly air. It's just like this was all my place, Darrell thought. Like I was by myself here and owned every little thing.

One of the herons flew over his head. There was the rushing sound of wind through its great feathers and it grumbled gently in its deep buzzy voice as it went. Darrell grinned, watching the bird circle and land on the barn roof to look down on him.

"And them old cranes too," he told himself. "And I'll

catch me one if I want too. I'll go fix up them ropes and catch me one."

He dropped the fork and started off. But then he stopped. The old man could see him out the window, he knew. He wasn't going back in that house and let the old geezer nag him about not finishing things. He knew how to work. He might not like it, but he knew how and he could do it as well as a man. He finished the row and did half the next. The turnips filled the basket. He'd do the rest some other time.

He knocked the dirt from the pick and the fork and took them back into the barn. He carried the turnips to the house door and set them down, but he didn't go in. He hadn't been near the river since the old man had been laid up and it made him feel kind of good to see it there, going along, calm and steady, and making its lapping and gurgling noises just like always. And just like always a fish leaped, coming down with a sharp crack and sending out circle after circle of rippling water.

Way up the island he could see one of the herons knee-deep in the river, still-hunting, leaning forward with its neck stuck out till it looked like the pictures of giraffes in the *Geographic* magazines. It stood there and never moved a muscle until Darrell grew tired of watching and went back after the ropes. He was disappointed about the ropes. There didn't seem to be nearly as much of them as there had been when the old man strung them up to dry clothes on. But he did the best he could with them.

He made a noose and laid it on the river bank with the loose end leading to a bush where he could hide and wait. The rest he tangled in and out of the trees and bushes. He had imagined the ropes would make a kind of net that would be sure to catch a bird. But now he was afraid he couldn't catch anything with these. He kept looping the ropes here and there, hoping to get some better arrangement.

A man went by in a motorboat. He was looking toward the island. The wind ruffled his red hair. When he saw Darrell, he raised his hand in greeting. Darrell just stared, standing there with the ropes dangling all around him. The man traveled on up the river but he turned his head to watch the boy until he was nearly out of sight.

"Let him look," muttered Darrell. "Maybe he'll go tell the law on me and come take the old man off to jail." Or would they? Even while he was sick would the uncle be responsible for what Darrell did?

Darrell shrugged. No matter what happened, likely he'd get off the island. He'd end up in some kind of home or orphanage. He wouldn't have to go to jail. He could run away from any kind of home ever built. He'd get away. He passed the end of the last rope through the branches of a button bush and set out for the house.

Next day the old man was up. He moved slowly and cautiously but he was up and cooked breakfast. "I had to get up," he said sourly. "I couldn't stand no more of your bread."

Darrell flared up. "You ate a mighty lot of it," he cried hotly. "If you didn't like it how come you ate so much of it?"

"Humph," said the old man. He had his back to his nephew but in the dented side of the coffeepot Darrell got a glimpse of his reflected face and it seemed like he was grinning. Darrell was mad. How come he had to bite on whatever the old dumbbell stuck out at him?

He was sitting at the table sulking when the old man looked out over the misty island and said suddenly, "Well, yonder they come. We ain't got nothing to worry about now."

82

Darrell sprang up. "Who's coming?" he asked. "Where?"

The old man pointed. Over the cornfield there was a flock of big birds. Not anywhere near as big as those old cranes, but plenty big. Brown-bodied, black-necked birds who called out to each other now and then in deep sweet voices. Slowly with braking motions of their wings they wheeled and turned over the rows of corn and settled at last to the ground.

"What's them?" asked Darrell. "Ducks?"

"Naw," answered the old man. "Them's geese, wild geese."

Darrell stared out at them. Among the corn only their long black necks showed plainly, like the dark stalks of some kind of curious plant. Through the window he could hear the low continuous murmur of their voices. By and by, first one and then another bent to eat the corn spilled among the rows or still clinging to the dry cobs scattered here and there.

"You fixing to shoot one and eat it?" asked Darrell.

"Shoot one?" asked the old man. "With what? My big toe? I ain't got no gun. 'Sides, this is the Reserve."

83

"Well, then, how they going to be any help to you?" demanded Darrell. "You said now you ain't got nothing to worry about."

"I mean game warden'll be along any day now," the old man explained. "To check on how many's feeding here, and such as that."

"And find them ropes," said Darrell to himself. "If he don't know what they're for, I'll tell him. And then he can cart the old buzzard off to jail."

The game warden needn't know he'd done it while the old man was down in the bed. There wasn't anybody to say it hadn't been done a month ago.

Now he asked, "How'll the game warden know? I mean how'll he find out about the geese being here."

"He'll look to see," the old man said. "He goes up and down the river in a motorboat all the time. He'll be looking for 'em. He's got these big old glasses can see pretty nigh from here to China."

Darrell's heart gave a queer little jerk in his chest. That man in the boat, the one who had waved while he was putting up the ropes, that had been the game warden, he knew it. No telling how often the game warden had been watching him this winter.

The old man struck a match and began to suck on his pipe. The match burned clear down to his finger tips before he tried to light the tobacco. It was a trick he had that nearabout drove Darrell out of his mind. He didn't know why, it just did. Watching he got so mad he couldn't think straight. Tears rushed to his eyes and he stood up suddenly and bawled, "Well, you better hope he don't come. Because when he does come, you're going to jail—and me too, most likely!"

84

THE OLD MAN looked startled. "What do you mean?" he asked after a minute. "What you talking about?"

"You was the one said it," crowed Darrell. He was triumphant. It was worth anything to see his uncle look like that. "You said if I got in trouble, you'd be the one to go to jail. You said you was responsible."

The old man laid down his pipe. "I said I'd wallop you if you got in trouble, and I meant it," he said and his eyes turned the color of the river on a cold morning. "What you talking about?"

Darrell drew back a little. "I m-mean them old cranes," he stammered. "You thought you would get me in trouble, telling me to try to catch one. But you're the one that'll have to go to jail for it. You the one the game warden will be after. I got them ropes out there now to catch one. He'll see it."

The old man blazed up. "You mean you left my good ropes out in the weather all this time?" he yelled. "What's got into you? Them's good ropes, cost good money."

He tried to stand up and groaned and grabbed his back.

85

He slumped back in his chair and sat there mumbling to himself. Finally he picked up his pipe and pointed the stem end of it toward Darrell. "You know something? You ain't real smart. Didn't you ever take a look at one of them birds? Supposing you'd caught one with them ropes, what was you going to do about it? They ain't sparrows. They got wings that can knock a man down. And the first thing they go after with them big old beaks is a man's eyes. They could kill a boy like you easy as not."

Now it was Darrell's turn to look startled. He guessed he was pretty dumb. In Detroit there weren't any birds like that, birds that could kill you, birds that had laws made about them.

"Maybe I'm dumb," he said sullenly, "but I ain't done nothing but what you told me to. I never tried to get you in trouble or get your eyes pecked out or nothing."

The old man didn't answer. Together they sat watching the geese among the rows of corn. The black heads, marked with gleaming white cheek patches, stuck up here and there as one or another stopped feeding to scout for danger. Darrell got so interested in where the next head was going to pop up he forgot the quarrel. It came over him all of a sudden that he was sitting there staring at wild geese. He'd heard about wild geese most of his life and how they were things people didn't often get close up to. And here he was about near enough to a whole flock of them to reach out and touch them.

"Naw," said the old man suddenly and Darrell jumped. "You ain't dumb, not dumb at all. You're smarter than I was at your age, I reckon."

He rubbed his hand back and forth over his stubbly chin.

"Maybe you're a little bit smarter than me right now," he said and grinned. "I want you to know I didn't sick you on them old cranes to get you in trouble. It never came in my head to get you in trouble, specially not that kind of trouble. I'm sort of in charge here in this part of the Reserve and it's kind of up to me to see nothing bad happens to them cranes or the geese. It's kind of up to me to see don't nothing bad happen to you neither," he added.

"Well, like I say, maybe I ain't so smart as I ought to be. When I was a young 'un like you, one summer my grandpa promised me a quarter for catching one of them big old cranes. I never thought about catching one with a trap or a net nor nothing. I just ran after 'em like I'd run after one of my momma's fryers to kill for Sunday dinner. I chased them old fellers all summer long, kept me busy every waking minute I wasn't working. My arms must of growed a foot reaching out trying to lay hold of just one tail feather."

He laughed out loud and his eyes held a blank faraway look as though what he was seeing wasn't the house and the window's view of geese, but himself as a boy, running and racing along the river bank after the tall herons.

A minute later he went on. "Place like this, there ain't always a lot for a boy like you to do. Reckon I thought it'd help for you to be poling up and down after them birds the way I did. It just never entered my mind you might not do it the way I did. And that's sure not too bright, ever."

Darrell picked up the salt shaker from the table and held it tight in his fist. The old man had said he was smart! And he'd sort of halfway meant it.

87

"You go bring in them ropes," the uncle said suddenly. "Them's good ropes."

Darrell stood up. At the door he turned and asked, "You going to tell? You going to tell the game warden?"

The old man frowned at him. "Have to," he answered. "If I seen somebody else trying to catch them old cranes, I'd tell. Just 'cause it's you and me don't make no difference."

As he looped up the ropes, Darrell looked around for the herons. Now he didn't suppose he'd ever get a chance to catch one, any way at all. It was kind of a disappointment. It would have been exciting to do it. He would have liked to have one in a cage or something.

Instead here he was, likely in deep trouble with the law. And the herons were probably sitting in some tree, big and dignified as ever. They were smarter than either of the two human beings on this island. They weren't in any kind of trouble and nobody had come anywhere near catching one of them.

Two days later the door opened and the musselman walked in. "How come you ain't got me some coffee ready?" he asked the old man.

"'Cause I ain't got no coffee," the old man answered peaceably. "My coffee's over on the river bank, along with 'bout half the rest of my eats for the winter."

"No, it's not," the musselman answered. "I brought it all over. I figured you must be down sick or something. I hadn't seen you out and around. And this morning I saw that the door to your shack was open and I went and looked in the truck. So I loaded up all that stuff and brought it over. Brought you some ham too."

"Well, bring it in then," said the old man. "I been out of coffee for three days and I don't like it."

Darrell went on tying his shoes.

"That there's my nephew, Darrell, come to live with me," the old man added. "I reckon you already know him."

"We done met," the musselman said and grinned. "He's company for you, must be."

"Company!" snorted the old man. "He ain't nothing but trouble."

The visitor winked at Darrell. "He can come help me carry in them groceries anyhow," he pointed out.

"How long's he been down in the back?" asked the musselman when they were outside.

Darrell thought back. "Little over a week," he answered.

"Old bonehead!" exclaimed the musselman and laughed. "Kind of hard on an old man living out here in the middle of the river."

Later he ate breakfast with them. It was the best food Darrell had ever tasted. He had thought he was going to have to eat corn bread and turnips forever. Now they had ham and biscuits and two kinds of jam and lots of coffee. The old man made it strong. The musselman said it nearly melted his spoon, it was so strong. Actually Darrell didn't like coffee, and especially he didn't like the old man's coffee. But he wasn't going to let on in front of the old man or the musselman either. He put heaps of sugar and canned cream in his, trying to make it taste good.

When the fisherman had finished eating he pushed back his plate and said, "Reckon it's going to make a difference to you having somebody living here with you. Reckon there'll be some changes made."

"Like what?" asked the old man.

The musselman picked up his knife and pointed it at the old man. Blackberry jam dripped slowly from the blade.

"You got to get you a motorboat," he said solemnly.

The old man frowned. "What for?" he asked. "I get along fine with my old boat. She don't use no oil or gas, she don't conk out, and she don't make a racket."

"Well, I never said you had to give her up," answered the fisherman. "You got to get a motorboat too. It's going to be sometime before that boy can row across the river, specially in bad weather. He'll be going to school next fall. You going to row him back and forth twice a day? Or you going to let him learn how to handle a motorboat this summer so he can get hisself back and forth? Times when you're stove up in bed like this, is he going to set home and miss school?"

Darrell's head popped up. School! He hadn't thought about it. He didn't like school. Or he didn't used to. Now he found himself almost looking forward to it. At least he'd be getting away from the island and the old man. Of course, he'd be shut up all day with a bunch of dumb country boys. Still if there was just somebody there who wasn't too bad, he could make friends, maybe.

Anyway, he guessed he'd be the only one in school who lived on an island and got back and forth by himself in a motorboat every day. Darrell had a picture of himself dashing down the river in his speedy red boat, like the fishermen from the motel near the dam. He could hardly wait, all of a sudden, to start going to school.

The old man picked up his pipe and sucked on it. Then he shrugged. "Reckon he could manage all right. Raised in a city, like. Reckon he knows all about motors and engines and things." His voice was faintly scornful.

The musselman went on. "And it ain't just school. You got to think about other things. It's all right for you to lay

out here and die of pneumonia or a broke neck or something, but it ain't hardly fair to ask the boy to set by and die with you. He's got to have some way to get off the island if the need ever comes."

The old man turned and looked a long time at Darrell. Finally he said, "He can take care of hisself. He come all the way from Detroit without nobody with him. That's a long way for a boy to travel all alone." He made a horrible noise with the pipe. "Don't seem like he'd need a motorboat. But I can see you ain't going to listen to reason. If you think I got money to waste on motorboats, you go buy me one."

Darrell looked from one to the other. Did that mean he got the motorboat? Or not?

CHAPTER *9*

THE GEESE seemed to like it when it snowed. They kept standing up out of the corn, stretching and flapping their wings and honking. Darrell knew how they felt. He liked it too. Even in Detroit where the snow was grimy as soon as it hit the ground, he'd liked it. And here it was better.

The big flakes came down thick and fast, and it wasn't any time till the ground was covered. The bushes bent with snow and it made high white ridges along the smooth branches of the sycamores, so white the trees looked yellow in contrast. When the herons landed or took off, they sent big scoops of snow showering down.

When it stopped snowing, Darrell went outside. The geese had finished eating and were gone, flying back to join the others on an island a few miles upstream, the old man said. Darrell thought he'd like to go there some time. Ten thousand geese were a mighty lot of geese.

He reached out and scooped up a handful of snow off the top of a button bush. It was so light and fluffy and white, it looked good enough to eat. He took a bite and it was nothing, just a little cold and wet.

93

He went on to Mattie's pasture. A rabbit's track crossed one corner, otherwise the field lay as smooth and unmarked as water in a bucket. He looked at it for a minute and then whooped out and ran to throw himself face down in it.

The powdery cold stuff sprayed up all around him and he could feel it slide down the neck of his jacket. He got up carefully and there was his picture in the snow, arms and legs spread wide. He grinned. He'd always wanted to do that and he'd never before had a big enough patch of smooth clean snow.

He wished he had somebody to show it to. He moved over and did it again. The "whump" his body made as it hit the ground sounded loud as a thunderclap. How come the snow made everything sound so different, he wondered.

All the sounds were there, just like always—the water running and crows and jays calling and way down the river a dog barking. But they were all different, clear and set off by themselves somehow. It was funny.

Suddenly he got up and ran stumbling across the field as fast as he could and then flung himself down and rolled over and over yelling. One bad thing about Florida, they didn't have snow. Anybody who didn't like snow must be crazy.

He thought the snow would last a long time, but the sun came out and in twenty-four hours it was gone, except where it had drifted against the shady side of the house.

Now ain't that just my luck? he thought sourly, staring out at the gray fields and the bare trees and the harsh white sky. First good thing that's happened since I been here, and now look.

The old man stirred the black-eyed peas, simmering on the stove, and then whanged the spoon on the side of the pot.

"Turned out nice weather after all," he stated.

Darrell glowered.

"Reckon we'll go this afternoon," his uncle went on.

"Go where?" Darrell asked sulkily. But inside he was eager to leave. Going anywhere was better than staying here.

"Why, go buy that boat," answered the old man, sounding surprised that Darrell didn't know.

Darrell was glad he had his back turned so the old man couldn't see how startled and pleased he was. The old geezer was really going to buy a motorboat! Darrell got so excited he couldn't swallow.

He didn't let on to the old man, though. After a minute he muttered, "Well, you don't have to buy it for me."

"Naw, I reckon I don't," replied the uncle and went on opening a can of peaches.

By the time they left, Darrell was in such a tizzy he couldn't hide it. He was full of jitters. It was the first time the old man had tried any rowing since he hurt his back and about halfway over Darrell was scared to death they weren't going to make it.

The old man just sat in the skiff and let it go sliding downstream while he rested. But they got over at last. They landed way below the shack where the truck stayed, and Darrell had to pull the boat up on the bank all by himself, while his uncle stood there mumbling and holding his back.

Darrell started to point out that the old man would be having a hard time without him, and then he remembered if it wasn't for him the old man wouldn't be in such bad shape, and they wouldn't be crossing the river either. So he kept his mouth shut.

The dam didn't look the way he had expected it to. It was low and wide, instead of high and skinny. He sure did like riding along the top of it and looking down at the water. And he could see all those boats drawn up along the shore. He hadn't known there were so many boats in the world. All kinds, sailboats and cabin cruisers and motorboats, every size and color.

And more people than Darrell had seen since he got off the bus from Detroit.

The mussel fisherman was waiting for them. "It don't look like so much," he explained. "You could paint it if you felt like it. But it's a good boat, don't leak nowhere hardly, and the motor's fine. In good shape. I tried it out all up and down the river."

So Darrell had been warned. Still it jarred him when he finally laid eyes on the boat. Wouldn't you know it would be like that—a little bitty old wooden thing with green paint flaking off and a rusty motor wired to one end? The old man could have it. Darrell wasn't going to run it. He'd wait till he got to Florida and then he'd get himself a real boat, a flashing red speedboat with a motor all new and gleaming and powerful enough to lift the whole shebang right up out of the water. He would never chug along in a crummy looking thing like that.

The musselman got in and out of it and the old man heaved himself off the dock and down into it, but Darrell just squatted and stared disgustedly off over the river. He didn't notice anybody coming up till the man was right on him. He turned his head and looked up and it seemed like the newcomer was twelve feet tall and six feet wide. His hair was red.

It was the game warden. Darrell knew right away it was, and a little cold worm of worry began to gnaw at him.

"That's a good boat," said the game warden.

"I done told 'em that," the musselman spoke up. "I been up as far as the highway and back in it, and it's a good boat."

The game warden looked at the old man. "You fixing to run it?" he asked.

The old man shook his head. "Not if I can help it," he answered. He nodded toward Darrell. "He aims to drive

97

it, going to school and all. He's got to go to school next fall. Reckon he'll be with your youngest boy."

The game warden reached down and hauled the old man up on the dock.

"I heard you were bad off," said the warden. "But I figured you were too mean to die."

"I ain't been too pert," the old man admitted. "Things kind of got out of hand out there. Maybe you better come have a look."

He's fixing to tell about the cranes, Darrell thought. He'd just about made his mind up the old man was going to keep his mouth shut. He might not be scared of much, but Darrell hoped he'd be scared of going to jail and leaving the island and Mattie and everything.

How come he's buying a boat, if we both got to leave? he wondered bitterly. Well, I got better things to do with my time than go to jail or any old orphans' home or anything. I'll run off before then.

"I'll be out soon," the game warden said. "How many geese you reckon you got this winter? Thirty? Thirty-five? If I live I mean to band those critters. Remember five years ago we banded nine? I want to see if any of them are still coming back."

"You think more of them geese than you do of folks," said the old man with a grin. "Here I was down in the bed and you never come near me."

The game warden grinned back. "I kept an eye on you," he said.

The old man took his wallet out of his pocket and peered into it like it was deep as a well and had a dime at the bottom. "I got to go buy a boat," he announced.

He and the musselman just walked off. Darrell didn't

know whether to follow or not. The game warden put a hand on his shoulder and Darrell jumped. It almost felt like being arrested.

"Come on over to my boat," the red-headed man said. "I'm waiting for my boy Joe. He'll be along in a few minutes. Maybe you'd like to get to know him."

Darrell went along. He didn't know what else to do, though he was sort of half-scared he'd forgotten how to talk to anybody his own age.

He walked easy. After all a game warden was a kind of policeman. There wasn't any point being too friendly with him, but there wasn't any point getting him riled up either. Especially a policeman who'd been keeping an eye on you while you broke the law.

"You got just one boy?" Darrell asked politely.

"I've got three," answered the warden. "But two of them are nearly grown, in high school. Joe's eleven. That's about your age, isn't it? I reckon he'd give his eye teeth and a dollar to be living out there like you are. All my boys are crazy about that place. The oldest two used to camp out there a lot when they were coming up. And Joe's always pestering to do it. Reckon I'll have to bring him out sometime."

They had reached the game warden's boat. It was a shining red-and-white fast-looking boat with a heavy powerful-looking motor. Darrell could hardly stand to think about that shabby green wreck the old man was buying.

Darrell looked the boat over carefully. "Where's your gun?" he asked.

The game warden was surprised. "I've got a couple of guns at home," he said, "but I don't often take 'em around with me."

"Well, suppose you meet somebody doing something wrong, hurting the birds or something," said Darrell. "I mean like trying to catch one of them big old cranes."

"I've got a *badge*," answered the warden. "I don't need a gun. Anyway it's not the herons I have to watch out for so much. It's the geese and ducks."

"You mean if somebody tried to catch one, sort of by accident or something, you wouldn't arrest them?" asked Darrell.

"It would depend," said the red-headed man. "Yonder comes Joe."

Joe was red-headed too. He was swinging along on crutches with one foot in a cast.

"What's the matter with him?" Darrell burst out, though his daddy had always said it wasn't good manners to ask about things like that.

"Broke his foot," answered the game warden. "Fell in a ditch chasing after his goat."

"Goat!" cried Darrell. He didn't remember ever seeing a real live goat. It was funny, and yet it was kind of— well, it made Darrell feel impressed. A goat was a kind of wild thing, like a bear, it seemed to him.

"An old lady gave him a little nanny," the game warden went on. "She's a cute little thing, but she's not easy to keep up with. He wants to get a herd, but I don't see how he can when he can't even keep up with one nanny. And anyway he's got chickens and a dog and rabbits. He doesn't need goats. And he had to give up playing basketball at school on account of his foot."

Joe came hopping up. He grinned at Darrell and said, "Hi!" When his father said Darrell would be in school with him in the fall, Joe said, "Gee, great," but he didn't

100

sound too enthusiastic. It wasn't till he found out where Darrell lived that he grew interested. His eyes lit up and Darrell could tell he was envious. He must be off his rocker, Darrell thought. Maybe living out there was better than living in Detroit, a little bit. But it wasn't nearly as good as living in Florida.

"I been out there a lot," said Joe. "That big old mud puppy still living in the watering trough?"

"Sure," answered Darrell though he wasn't sure what a mud puppy was.

"That's the best place," Joe went on admiringly. "Once I was out there and the water was so high it was right up to the barn, nearly."

"It'll likely go that high next month," put in his father.

"Can I go out then?" asked Joe. "Can I, Pop?"

"Maybe," answered the warden. "If I can get things straightened out by then."

He means if he can get me arrested and off to jail by then, thought Darrell. I don't reckon he wants his boy hanging around with somebody bad like me.

Well, he didn't care. He could live without Joe and his stupid old goat. He could live without the game warden too. It didn't make any difference to him what they thought of him. Maybe when he got to Florida he'd rob a bank and they'd find out how bad he really was.

Only he sure would like to get one look at that goat. Did a nanny have horns? Sharp ones?

"Gee, you're lucky," said Joe and clambered down into the boat. "Come on, Pop," he called. "I got to get home!"

"I'll be out in a day or two," the game warden told Darrell. "Don't let anything happen to my birds."

He got in the boat and started it off. Joe grinned

and waved. He looked like a good guy. He looked like a friend.

I wish I'd caught one of them cranes, thought Darrell fiercely. As long as I got to go to jail anyway, here when I'm just getting a boat and getting to know guys, I wish I'd gone on and caught one!

He and the musselman took the boat back to the island. The musselman made him do the driving. At first he didn't want to. Crummy old boat. But then he did and it was kind of fun. The motor could push along better than he'd given it credit for. It could really travel and the spray rose up around him in a white wall.

The wind was just cold enough to feel good, blowing his hair back and whipping around his ears. He grinned at the musselman as they jounced over the water. He hadn't known it would be this much fun.

Running a motorboat was easy, once you got on to how to start the thing. He could manage by himself any time.

He didn't have to stay here and be arrested! He could leave any old day, he thought suddenly. He could go to Florida or any place. He didn't ever have to stay on that island any more.

In a way it was kind of sad. He wouldn't mind seeing whatever it was the game warden was going to do to the geese. He'd like to stay that long. And he'd like to be there when Joe came out to visit. And just for a while he'd like to go to school, to be the boy who lived on an island and came to school in his own boat.

But he didn't have much choice. It was leave or get thrown in jail or some home or other. It didn't matter much. Wherever he went he could take care of himself, he was certain.

102

Almost certain. He could find somewhere to live and some way to get along. He'd have to.

He opened the throttle wide and the spray of drops grew higher. Just any time now and he'd be gone from this place forever!

CHAPTER 10

THE OLD MAN was up on the barn roof. "Bring me up that roll of tar paper," he bawled down to Darrell. "And be careful. I ain't got time for broke legs this morning."

Darrell steadied the roll over his shoulder and went slowly up the ladder. "That old hen you was looking for," he said. "I seen her in the lean-to, in a bucket."

The old man whanged in two or three tacks before he answered. "Trying to nest, I reckon," he said. "I'll get me a setting of eggs under her soon as I can."

Darrell remembered seeing baby chickens in dime stores around Easter. They were cute. "You raise a lot of chickens?" he asked.

The old man shook his head. "Not too many. I just raise my laying chickens. I buy my eating chickens. The ones I hatch ain't hardly enough for laying even. Possums and hawks get 'em, and they drown their fool selves. We'll have to do better this year. Maybe you could kind of keep an eye on 'em. Now you watch out. You're fixing to fall off."

Darrell glared. "I ain't fell off nothing yet," he snapped.

"What for you always waiting around for me to do something wrong?"

"Because it's a boy's nature to do something wrong," answered the old man. "When I was your age I was doing something wrong every living minute of the day. Come over here and help me get this paper unrolled."

Scrambling over the sloping roof they unrolled the sticky black paper. Darrell held it while the old man tacked. The sun was warm and the wind wasn't too cold. At the far end of the cornfield the geese stood watching. They were used to these two human beings and didn't pay them much attention ordinarily. But having them up on the barn roof was strange and maybe dangerous and the geese watched.

Looking the other way Darrell could see Mattie grazing peacefully in her meadow, one of the herons in the sycamore tree, and another standing in the water, way over on the other side of the river. It was so far away and still, he might have thought it was just a stump. Only he knew it wasn't by the way its back shone steely blue-gray when the sun touched it. And once it turned its head so that he could see its big yellow beak and the ragged white feathers along its neck.

The heron rose and flew off. Darrell watched a boat come slowly down the river. He had an idea it was the game warden. He craned his neck as the boat slid out of sight behind the trees. His own boat was there.

"You can let go of the paper, I got it nailed down ten minutes ago," said the old man. "You go on down and tell the game warden I'll be down in a spell."

Darrell snatched his hands off the paper and glared.

This was the third time the game warden had been here

in a week. So far Darrell had managed to stay out of sight. Now he reckoned he wouldn't be able to. He'd have to face up to any trouble that was coming. He climbed slowly down the ladder.

The sound of the motorboat died to a series of dull pops. With a sudden wild clamor the geese rose in the air and circled overhead. When they had gone, the old man yelled down, "Go in the house and stir them black-eyed peas. I don't want 'em to burn!"

"Stir 'em yourself," muttered Darrell. But he did as he was told. The house was warm and full of light. Samuel was asleep in the old man's chair, and Darrell stroked his hand along the cat's back as he passed. Samuel stretched and yawned and Darrell grinned.

He stirred the peas then he went out again and down to the river. The game warden's boat was full of stuff, a big net, and pieces of old tires and things.

When he heard Darrell, the warden looked up and waved. "Oh, how beautiful heaven must be if it's any more beautiful than Tennessee in the springtime," he called.

"It ain't spring!" Darrell said, surprised.

"Sure it is," the red-headed man answered. "Take a look up the mountainside there." Darrell looked. It was funny he hadn't noticed it before, the way the trees were blurred with a thin faint haze of pink and gold. And even a little green here and there.

"I've got a crazy little wild plum tree at my place in full bloom," said the warden, beginning to pull the net out of the boat. "That's how come I want to get these geese banded right away, if I'm going to do it. Just any time now they're liable to remember they have better things to do up north. Lend me a hand here."

106

Darrell helped him carry the net and the pieces of tires. They took everything to the far end of the cornfield, where the geese were most likely to come. The warden cut the fence at that end of the field.

"Now what you up to?" asked the old man, walking up. "Looks like you could of asked me before you go cutting up my good fence."

"It was rotten anyway," the game warden answered. "See there where it's rusted plumb in two? You and the boy can put up another one. Give you something to do."

"Ain't you got nothing to worry you but how to use up my time?" asked the old man. He began to help wind up the rusty wire.

"I'll spread the corn around here good and thick," explained the game warden. "I'll fix the net and lay the fuses for the dynamite caps. Then keep the livestock away from here. It's dangerous in the first place, and I don't want anything to go wrong in the second place. I want those geese."

"I ain't livestock," burst out Darrell.

The game warden looked astonished. "I never said you were," he pointed out, and the look on his face made it plain he thought eleven-year-old boys had sense enough not to mess with things that weren't any of their business.

He made Darrell help him drive five tall stakes in a semi-circle around the scattered corn. The stakes slanted inward. One side of the net was fastened to the ground just behind the stakes and the net itself folded and draped over them, with the weights attached to the free side. The warden was very fussy that the weights, pieces of old tractor tires, should be in just the right places.

Darrell wanted to see where the dynamite caps went

that blew the whole business up in the air and over the geese. But the game warden sent him to the boat for some wire clippers and when he got back the job was finished and the game warden was covering up the fuse wires with dry leaves and grass.

"This is for the geese, ain't it?" Darrell asked suddenly, and the game warden nodded. "Well, how about them cranes, them herons, I mean? Don't you never try to get one of them?"

The game warden scratched his head. "I'd like to," he admitted. "Not too many of them get banded. Mostly young ones still in the nest. There isn't any way to draw herons to a net, like you can geese and ducks with corn." He pondered a minute. "I might try to get one at night. Let's go look at that tree they roost in."

"Okay," said Darrell.

The old man wouldn't come. "I done seen that tree," he said, and went back to the barn.

The sun was growing really hot. As they crossed Mattie's field the wet earth and the grass were warm underfoot. Darrell glanced down. There was a greenish tint to the growing things and there were flowers blooming. Tiny little white and purple things, but flowers just the same.

"How you coming along with the motorboat?" the man asked.

"I can handle it pretty good," answered Darrell. And he could.

"When my oldest boy goes off to state college next fall, Joe wants to take over his trotlines," the game warden said. "I don't think he's going to have time. Maybe you could do it, or anyway part of them. They don't bring in much money, but a little is more than nothing."

And that was the truth, Darrell well knew. If he was

going to stay he'd like to do it. But he wasn't going to stay. He was going to leave as soon as he could.

They came to the sycamore tree where the herons roosted. The game warden walked all around it and looked it over, rubbing his chin as he went. "I don't know. There're ways to do this, but I haven't got the equipment. You just don't walk up and put your hand on a big blue heron. I guess you found that out?"

For just a second Darrell was scared, he didn't know why. He'd been pretty sure all along the game warden knew what he'd been doing all winter. "You going to arrest me?" he asked finally.

"I reckon not," he said. "No harm's been done. I don't think you even meant to do any harm, when you get down to it. I guess everybody's entitled to do a few stupid things in his life."

"I ain't stupid," muttered Darrell. But then he figured he had been pretty dumb. He should have known he couldn't get one of those big birds—not with a rock or a rope or anything.

He'd meant to harm the old man, though. He'd almost forgotten why. Just because he'd had to come and live on this crazy old island, he reckoned, and he wanted to make somebody sorry for it.

"Anyway I been in jail all winter," he said suddenly. "Couldn't go nowhere or see nothing."

The game warden laughed. "That bad?" he asked. "Well, we're even then. You didn't really break the law and I didn't really send you to jail. I guess things'll be a lot better from now on."

They sure will, thought Darrell. I can leave here now and things sure will get better. I can leave the game warden and the cranes and the island and the old man . . .

"How about him?" he asked. "The old man. Will he have to go to jail? He kind of figured he might on account of he put me up to it. And he's looking after me."

"No harm's been done," repeated the game warden. "I'm not fixing to put anybody in jail. But first time you do something you shouldn't, I'll be on you quick."

He would too, Darrell could tell. It didn't matter. He was going to leave pretty soon. Next week, maybe, after the geese were banded. Or whenever he wanted to.

But he was glad the old geezer didn't have to go to jail. Going to jail might be hard on an old man like that. And anyway somebody had to look after the chickens and Samuel and Mattie.

Still it was a shame nobody had been able to lay a finger on those cranes. Darrell still thought it would be a great thing to do. And he just might get his picture in the paper if he could do it. And on TV.

"Here's where my boys used to camp," said the warden, pointing.

Darrell looked. "How come your boys were so crazy about coming out here?" he asked suddenly. "What did they *do*?"

"Well, it isn't everybody can say they've lived on an island in the middle of the river," explained the red-headed man. "They just liked being here. Outdoors where its quiet and peaceful-like. They used to fish and watch for deer up the mountain there. There're plenty of deer around here."

He ran a hand down the smooth white trunk of the sycamore. "I guess one thing they like is being on their own and by themselves. That's kind of a good feeling, don't you think? You like to think you can do it."

Darrell thought about it. It *was* kind of a good feeling.

110

It was like those mornings when he had fed Mattie and tended to things all by himself. He guessed he was as good at getting along by himself as anybody, even his uncle said so.

The game warden started back across the field with Darrell at his heels. "You know how boys are," he went on. "They think they've got to have radios and cars and excitement. Well, everybody worth shooting ought to be able to get along for a while without anything but just themselves and some dry matches. It's a lot more fun."

Suddenly he stopped and stared up into the sky. Darrell looked up too. At first the sun was too bright for him to see. But he could hear. Something was up there, screaming in a wild fierce voice. It shrieked again and again.

"There!" said the game warden. "Look yonder. Three of them."

On steady outspread wings the herons circled the sun, three of them, one after the other in soaring widening circles. The air blazed with those strange harsh screams. Around and around, high and remote and unreal in the sun's white ring. And then suddenly one of them dived. With a deep rushing singing sound, like a great kite falling, it plunged down and down and down.

It was going to hit the ground! It was going to crash! Darrell started to yell, and then the heron opened its partly folded wings and swooped up over his head, in a rush, in a storm of feathers and wings that almost knocked him off his feet. One of the others shrieked twice more and then they were gone, all three of them.

Darrell looked around dazedly, half-blinded by the sun and by the wonder of what he had seen. "What—what was that?" he asked.

"Courting," answered the game warden after a minute. "That's their courting dance. They're getting ready to leave here and choose mates and make nests. I told you spring was here. I'm glad I got after those geese today."

"Do they go far away?" he asked.

"Hundred miles or so," answered the warden. "The geese go a right smart piece further than that. But they'll be back. They always come back."

For a minute Darrell was sorry he wasn't going to be there to see them. He'd like to see that old crane dive like that again. It had made him feel almost like he'd felt that time he rode the roller coaster.

112

The old man was back up on the roof when they got to the house. The game warden hollered up that he'd be back early in the morning, really early. The old man just went on tacking.

Darrell climbed back up the ladder till his head was on a level with the old man's heels. "Want me to help?" he asked finally.

The old man drove in a nail with four blows of his hammer. The whacks grew louder, one after the other, and sent an echo running up the hills on the other side of the river.

"Naw," he answered in the sudden silence. "I'm done. Let's git on down. It flusters me to have you climbing around on this roof. You're bound to break your neck sooner or later."

To show how good he was at breaking his neck, Darrell jumped off the fourth rung of the ladder and nearabout jarred his teeth out. But he pretended it didn't hurt. He bent over to pick up some of the scattered tar paper to keep the old man from seeing how red his face got from the pain.

The old man whacked him on the bottom. "How come you still wearing those blue jeans?" he asked. "They're about wore through in the seat. And they're tight enough to saw you in two. How come you don't wear those new ones I bought you?"

Darrell straightened up and looked the old man right in the eye. "I can get along with what I come here with," he said. "I may be nothing but trouble to you, but you don't have to buy me no clothes or nothing."

"What you mean—nothing but trouble?" asked the old man.

"You told him that, you told the musselman," Darrell

113

cried. "He said I was company for you, and you said I wasn't nothing but trouble."

The old man stared at him. "Haw!" he snorted. "Reckon I did. You're trouble. But ain't trouble the best kind of company there is? Get in the house and get you some decent clothes on!"

CHAPTER 11

THE LIGHT of the lamp woke Darrell. He lay listening to the voices of the old man and the game warden mumbling every now and then. The coffee smelled good and after a while he climbed out of bed.

The game warden grinned at him. "Hurry up. Get you some breakfast and get dressed. We've got work to do."

It was getting light when they left the house. The game warden hurried Darrell along. "We ate too much," he complained. "We should have been out there twenty minutes ago."

The old man wouldn't come. "I ain't fixing to set out there and freeze my feet just to see you throw a net over some fool birds," he said and opened the door and flung out all the rest of the corn bread for the chickens.

Darrell thought maybe he was right. It was cold as Jee-rusalem. He had on his new jacket and it was warmer than his old jacket, but not warm enough. The wind off the river cut like a knife.

He and the game warden took their places in the bushes. The game warden kept fooling with the fuses and the box that set off the caps and worrying for fear it wouldn't work.

"It's pretty old," he explained. "It doesn't always work. But I reckon new things don't always work either."

The bushes sheltered them a little, but Darrell's ears and fingers stung sharply. "Good thing we ate a lot," the game warden muttered. "Bacon and corn bread are the best things I know to keep out the cold, if you eat enough of 'em."

"I wish I had some hot corn bread right now," said Darrell. "I'd put my feet on it."

The sky turned redder and redder, the black tangle of trees stood out to the last twig, the river flamed and brightened, and still the geese didn't come.

"Don't worry," said the game warden. "They'll be here. Unless they see the net and decide it's something waiting to grab them. Even then some of them will come on in. They're suspicious but they're mighty curious. And they don't like to change their ways. Once they get used to eating in a place, they like to keep up the custom."

The sun was up. Darrell figured he was frozen doubled up this way and wouldn't ever be able to unbend.

"I'm going to bring my Joe out here next week," the game warden went on. "He's got two days off from school and he wants to come, if he can think of something to shut that little nanny in while he's gone."

Darrell hardly knew what to think about Joe. He figured the game warden's boy must be all right. When he went to school next fall he wouldn't mind knowing another boy. If he went to school. He guessed he would. He wasn't going to have any money or anything to run off with this year.

He wished he had something to show Joe, like a goat.

116

He had his boat, but he figured Joe would be used to boats.

He had the island. You might say it was his island. He lived here. He knew every inch of it, as good as owned it, fields and barn and all. He had those old cranes, those big blue herons. He bet nobody else anywhere had ten or twelve of them beating back and forth overhead all day. Maybe one or two, but not this many, hanging around all the time. They were every bit as good as goats.

And he had the old man, of course. The old man was wild, a little bit, you might say, like a goat or a bear or a buffalo. If the game warden's boys thought it was something special to be able to get along by yourself without anything the uncle was mighty near a prize specimen. He grinned a little. He was sort of proud of the old geezer.

Come to think of it, he was kind of proud of himself, too. He could get along by himself without anything, almost. Those boys back in Detroit, the ones he used to run around with, he thought suddenly, they couldn't do it. They couldn't have spent the winter here the way he had, and taken care of the place and learned to be on his own.

"Look yonder," said the man. "There they come."

The geese circled. One of them had fallen behind the others and it called out reproachfully as it followed. They dropped and braked and landed, one after the other, disappearing into the corn.

"They ain't nowhere near the net," whispered Darrell.

"They will be," the game warden answered.

And sure enough in a little while they came edging out, long-legged and tall. The sun made their brown backs glow like brass. They came cautiously toward the net and lowered their black necks and began to eat the corn. Darrell counted. Five, twelve, nineteen . . .

117

"Reckon that's it," murmured the game warden and moved his hand to push down the plunger that would set off the charge.

"Wait," whispered Darrell. He had seen the great blue heron sitting in the tree watching. He didn't know how he could tell it was going to fly down and join the geese, but he knew. Speaking in its toad voice, growling and complaining to itself, it flapped its long wings and sailed out of the tree and down to the cornfield.

Darrell's heart thumped and bumped in his chest. They were going to catch it! He was going to get that heron and not have to go to jail for it. He'd make that old man pay him that dollar, or half of it anyway. He'd done half the catching.

The heron stalked slowly forward. The long reach of its shadow behind it made it look bigger than ever. There was a little fringe of reddish feathers down its throat, along with the white ones, and the great plumes on its head curved proudly out and back, like a crown, Darrell thought. Like it was king of the world.

Was it close enough now for the net to fall over it when it was triggered? Darrell held his breath. The heron halfway opened its wings, humping its shoulders up around its neck and then suddenly shoving them back and letting its wings close again. One of the geese walked in front of it and the heron stepped back.

Was it going to come close enough? Darrell could hardly keep himself from getting up and running over there to push the big bird up to the net. Oh, it had to come close enough!

He wished the old man was here. He'd give anything if the old man was here to see this crane get caught. Oh, he was going to have something to brag about now. He was going to put this bird in a cage and make the old man walk out and say "How do" to it, night and morning. He was going to get his picture in the paper and be on TV . . .

The heron turned its head quickly from side to side. The sun caught its big light eyes. It took three steps forward.

"Now!" yelled the game warden. There was an explosion that cracked over the river, a turmoil of wings, a crawling confusion of nets and birds, frantic honks, and a storm of feathers. Eight geese and something else sprang up into the morning. The game warden jumped to his feet. Darrell ran forward, and all of a sudden there was somebody standing beside him.

It was the old man. Like the heron he towered bigger and taller than natural. And then he laughed out. "Haw!" he bawled. "Never touched a hair!"

The eight escaped geese went screaming off down the river, the ones in the net lay still, once in a while uttering a pathetic honk.

But up over the sycamores, calmly, with vast smooth strokes of its great wings, the heron soared, free and light, higher and higher, the king of the world. Darrell could feel his own heart lift and sail with every long sure pull of those wings. Up and up, further and further, triumphant. Free.

And all at once he was glad. All at once he was laughing too. "Never touched a hair!" he echoed. "Never touched a hair!"

ABOUT THE AUTHOR

WILSON GAGE is the pen name of Mary Q. Steele, one of a family of gifted and successful writers; her husband, William, her sister, and her mother, Christine Govan, are the authors of many popular books for children and young people.

Wilson Gage was born in Chattanooga, Tennessee, and is a graduate of the University of Chattanooga where she received a bachelor's degree in physics and mathematics. Her long interest in nature—for which she confesses an "unathletic" love—and in regional history has characterized all of her books, most recently *Dan and the Miranda* and *Miss-Osborne-the-Mop*. She has three children and lives in Signal Mountain, Tennessee.

ABOUT THE ARTIST

GLEN ROUNDS' first collaboration with Wilson Gage, on *A Wild Goose Tale*, sprang from a shared fascination with nature and her small creatures.

Mr. Rounds was born in the South Dakota Bad Lands and grew up on a Montana ranch "well stocked with horses, cattle, gray wolves, badgers, antelope and the like." He attended the Art Institute in Kansas City, Missouri, and the Art Students League in New York, and has written and illustrated many books for children. His most recent is *Rain in the Woods and Other Small Matters*. He now lives in Southern Pines, North Carolina.